The Cursed C

Magnum Tenebr

CW00552273

The Cursed Canvas

Foreword

By

Magnum Tenebrosum

The Cursed Canvas

Dear Reader,

Prepare yourself, for you stand at the precipice of a chilling abyss, ready to descend into the darkness that lurks within the cursed canvas and the eldritch horrors that dwell beyond. I, Magnum Tenebrosum, serve as your guide into this abyss, a realm where the distinction between reality and nightmare is fragile at best.

As the author of this relentless descent into madness, I must provide a menacing warning. This narrative is not a mere tale spun from the depths of imagination; it is a chronicle of cosmic horror, an unholy symphony of terror, and the echoes of ancient malevolence. Its whispers will linger long after the last word has been read.

The cursed painting, an insidious portal to otherworldly horrors, demands your attention and offers no solace. It is not a work of art but a gateway to the darkest recesses of the human psyche, and it hungers for your acknowledgment.

You, dear Reader, are not a mere observer but an active participant in this unfolding nightmare. The curse that binds these words is no simple fiction; it is a relentless force, a malevolent entity that seeks to ensnare your mind and soul. Once it has you within its grasp, it will not let go, and the line between your reality and the eldritch will blur until you can no longer distinguish one from the other.

As you traverse this sinister tale, be prepared for the unsettling, the macabre, and the inexplicable. The curse has its designs, and its echoes may continue to haunt your reality long after turning the final page. The tendrils of its influence may reach out when you least expect it, and you will forever question the boundary between the real and the nightmarish.

Understand that your curiosity may be your ultimate undoing. The cursed painting beckons from the shadows, and its malevolent force is bound to intertwine with your psyche, forever changing your perception of reality. Your journey will be fraught with horrors that defy reason, nightmares that infiltrate your waking hours, and the relentless pursuit of forbidden knowledge.

As you tread the path of the Lovecraftian, where sanity is but a fragile veneer, remember there is no turning back. You have entered the realm of the enigma, a world where cosmic terrors wait in the shadows, their tendrils of dread ever-reaching.

With trepidation and the foreboding of things unseen,

Magnum Tenebrosum

Prologue

The Vision

The Cursed Canvas

In the darkest recesses of the night, beneath a veil of foreboding shadows, the artist Victor Marlowe found himself ensnared within the inescapable clutches of a dream that defied all reason and sanity. This was a dream that would forever haunt the corridors of his mind, a sinister prelude to a nightmare that would consume his waking life, dragging him into the abyss of unending cosmic horror.

His eyes, veiled in darkness, beheld an otherworldly realm where dimensions coalesced and realities twisted like the kaleidoscope of a fevered mind. It was a place where the laws of physics surrendered to the whims of malevolent cosmic forces, and the very fabric of existence unraveled at the seams. A malignant sky loomed overhead, punctuated by monstrous, cyclopean stars that pulsed with eldritch energy, casting grotesque, shifting shadows that danced to the eerie rhythm of despair.

Unearthly, iridescent hues painted the horizon, casting an eerie, sickly pallor over the dreamer's surroundings. The air seemed pregnant with malice, thick and suffocating as if the atmosphere were an ancient, sentient entity bearing witness to a reality that should never have been. The colors of this nightmarish panorama defied earthly description, existing on a spectral spectrum that straddled the boundaries between madness and revelation.

The Cursed Canvas

Amidst this nightmarish landscape, a grotesque entity manifested. It writhed and twisted, a grotesque amalgamation of limbs and tendrils, its fluid and solid form, a mockery of existence. It was as if the rules of anatomy had been shattered, and flesh and bone had been woven into a grotesque tapestry of madness. The entity's form undulated with a repulsive elegance, like a dance of cosmic horror, a perverse waltz through the corridors of the impossible.

Its eyes, an array of unblinking orbs, radiated an unsettling luminescence, revealing glimpses of forbidden knowledge that no mortal should ever know. Within those orbs lay the collective horrors of eons, the unending abyss that gazed back at Victor Marlowe from the depths of the cosmos. To meet the entity's gaze was to peer into the heart of madness itself, to touch the forbidden fruit of knowledge that lay at the core of existence.

Victor Marlowe's heart raced as he watched this abomination from a vantage point he couldn't comprehend. He stood on a precipice of reality, a fragile island of stability amidst the chaotic sea of the incomprehensible. The entity's presence exuded an overwhelming aura of malevolence, an aura that permeated the very essence of the dream. It was as if the dream rebelled against the intrusion of this eldritch horror, a testament to the fragility of the human mind in the face of cosmic forces beyond comprehension.

He was but a silent, powerless observer in this surreal theater of horrors, a helpless witness to the impending doom that hung like a spectral shroud over this eldritch landscape. Sensing his presence, the grotesque entity turned its abominable visage toward him, and at that moment, a cacophony of whispers, half-mad incantations from long-forgotten tongues, filled Victor's ears.

The words seemed to burrow into his mind, an invitation into a world of madness, beckoning him to embrace the unfathomable knowledge hidden within the depths of that nightmarish vision. It was a knowledge that promised both enlightenment and damnation, a revelation that could shatter the boundaries of human understanding. The whispers echoed through the labyrinthine corridors of his consciousness, insinuating themselves like tendrils of an invasive vine, binding him to the eldritch truth.

With a sudden jolt, Victor Marlowe awoke, drenched in cold sweat, his heart pounding. The vision faded, but the indelible mark of that cosmic horror had been seared into his psyche, forever etching its insidious presence into the recesses of his thoughts. The nightmare had only just begun, and Victor Marlowe knew, even then, that what he had glimpsed was but the first brushstroke in a maddening masterpiece of despair, a foreboding omen that would lead him into the inescapable abyss of "The Cursed Canvas." He had been chosen by forces beyond his understanding, marked by a revelation that would plunge him into madness and despair. As the first tendrils of dawn's light pierced the veil of night, he could not escape the knowledge that he was now a participant in a cosmic drama, with the stage set for horrors beyond imagination.

Part I

The Nightmares

Chapter 1

Fragile Sanity

The Cursed Canvas

In the dimly lit sanctuary of his studio, Victor Marlowe stood on the precipice of madness, his mind a turbulent sea of creativity and torment. He was a man who walked a tightrope between genius and insanity, and this delicate balance defined his existence. His name was celebrated in the art world, known for his macabre and surreal creations, but for those who knew him intimately, there was a haunting truth beneath the accolades – the truth of a soul irrevocably scarred by the art he had wrought.

Victor was in his early forties, though his haggard visage appeared far older. His once-handsome features had grown gaunt and pallid, his eyes dulled with the weight of the horrors he had seen. Deep lines etched across his forehead and around his eyes told the story of countless sleepless nights, each marked by the relentless pursuit of a vision only he could fathom. His obsidian hair, once vibrant, had faded to a disheveled gray, and his slender frame bore the marks of a life lived on the fringes of human experience.

His studio reflected his inner turmoil, a haven and a prison intertwined. Canvases covered in half-finished masterpieces leaned against the walls, their twisted, surreal forms hinting at the chaotic landscape of his psyche. The room bore the scent of paint and despair, a heady mixture that hung like a curse. Easels stood as sentinels, their blank canvases awaiting the touch of his tormented hand.

The studio was a sanctuary but also a prison, where the boundary between imagination and reality blurred and where the darkest corners of his mind were laid bare. Shadows danced upon the walls, cast by the dim glow of his solitary desk lamp as if the room itself pulsed with an eerie life of its own.

The nightmares, those insidious harbingers of doom, began as faint ripples in the ocean of his consciousness. They were visions that fluttered on the periphery of his awareness, elusive and haunting. In these early dreams, he wandered through landscapes that defied earthly description, standing on the precipice of uncharted realms. There was an unsettling familiarity to these dreams, a sense that they were not born of his own subconscious but glimpses into something ancient and unknowable.

He recognized the architecture of forgotten civilizations and heard the whispers of cosmic entities in a language that defied terrestrial comprehension. The dreams collided with the familiar and the eldritch, a disorienting blend of the known and the unfathomable. He could feel the pull of these dreamscapes, an irresistible gravity that drew him deeper into their arcane mysteries.

The Cursed Canvas

At the heart of these nascent nightmares, an entity, dark and formless, beckoned him with an insidious allure. It whispered forbidden secrets in forgotten tongues, promises of revelation that his conscious mind dared not confront. Its presence was a constant, an undercurrent that tugged at the fraying threads of his sanity. Sometimes, it took on a vague, indistinct shape, but its proper form remained tantalizingly beyond his understanding.

Victor's days were a facade of normalcy, a performance he enacted to navigate a world that had grown increasingly alien to him. Mundane routines masked the turmoil within, the gnawing unease that festered in the depths of his consciousness. He would talk with acquaintances, share smiles with colleagues, and attend art exhibitions where his work was hailed as visionary. But beneath the façade, his thoughts were consumed by the enigmatic entity from his dreams.

But it was in the night that the true horrors unfolded, as his dreams evolved into a surreal theater of cosmic dread. He would awaken in the dead of night, his body drenched in cold sweat, his heart pounding in his chest. The line between dream and reality blurred, and he couldn't shake the feeling that the entity from his nightmares was gradually encroaching upon his waking life.

The Cursed Canvas

Each morning brought a sense of disorientation, a haunting residue of the horrors that had unfolded in the night. His days were marked by a pervasive unease, a sense that he was being watched by unseen eyes. The entity had become an ever-present specter, a shadow that clung to his consciousness like a malignant parasite.

The initial nightmares were like a cruel overture, a prelude to the symphony of cosmic horror that would soon engulf his existence. They hinted at an entity that lurked just beyond the veil of his perception, a presence that was not content to remain confined to the realm of dreams. They were the first brushstrokes on the canvas of his torment, the opening notes of a symphony of madness.

As the nightmares grew in intensity and frequency, Victor Marlowe's grasp on reality slipped further. He questioned the nature of his existence, his sanity unraveling at the edges. It was as if the entity from his dreams had sunk its talons into his mind, inexorably pulling him into a chasm of cosmic horror from which there could be no escape. The artist was descending into the abyss and had only just glimpsed the first shades of darkness that awaited him.

He was haunted by a pervasive sense of being watched in his waking hours. It was as if the eyes of the entity from his nightmares followed his every move, lurking just beyond the periphery of his vision. He would catch fleeting glimpses of dark, shadowy figures in his peripheral vision, only to vanish when he turned to confront them. The boundary between his dreams and reality had eroded, and he could no longer discern where one ended and the other began.

Victor's art, once an expression of his creativity, had transformed into a conduit for the horrors that tormented him. The canvases, once blank slates for his vision, became portals to otherworldly realms, gateways to dimensions beyond human comprehension. Each completed painting was a descent into madness, a brushstroke that brought him closer to the abyss.

Once a sanctuary for artistic expression, the studio had become a chamber of horrors. Victor Marlowe was no longer in control; he was a pawn in a cosmic game played by forces he could not hope to understand. The entity's whispers grew louder, its promises more seductive, and the artist's resistance crumbled like fragile parchment.

He knew that he was teetering on the precipice of an abyss, that the line between

Creation and destruction had blurred entirely. The nightmares, once distant visions, had become a relentless onslaught, a symphony of madness that echoed in his every waking moment. The artist was descending into the abyss, and he knew that there was no turning back.

Chapter 2

The Awakening Abyss

The Cursed Canvas

The nightmares showed no mercy. Night after night, Victor Marlowe was drawn deeper into their malevolent grasp. His restless slumbers became an unending voyage into otherworldly realms, where reality warped and twisted into grotesque, surreal landscapes. The colors were beyond description, a riot of unearthly hues that defied the confines of human language. The air was thick with foreboding as if it bore the weight of impending doom.

In these dreams, the entity from his nocturnal terrors was no longer a distant specter; it was now an ever-present shadow, a sinister guest that loitered at the fringes of his consciousness. Its formless shape seemed to materialize from his psyche like a grotesque puppeteer pulling the strings of his sanity. It whispered secrets in ancient tongues, offering tantalizing glimpses into the forbidden knowledge that lay beyond the boundaries of human understanding. Its voice, a guttural and melodic symphony of madness, echoed in the recesses of his mind.

These dreams unfolded like chapters in a cosmic horror story. In one, Victor would find himself standing at the precipice of an alien city, its towering spires adorned with grotesque sculptures that seemed to writhe and contort in silent agony. In another, he would wander through forests of impossible geometry, where trees bore the fruit of forbidden wisdom, and the ground pulsed with an otherworldly heartbeat.

The nightmares escalated, each new night bringing a descent into more profound, more intricate layers of cosmic horror. Victor's waking hours became a mere intermission between the surreal theaters of his nocturnal journeys and the waking world. His studio, once a place of solace, had transformed into a nightmarish labyrinth where the boundaries between his art and the eldritch visions that tormented him blurred beyond recognition.

With each completed painting, the entity's influence over him grew more assertive. It was as if the dreams demanded an outlet, a way to manifest the abominable horrors that lurked within his subconscious. The canvas became his confessional, and the brush, his sacrificial instrument. His hand trembled as he picked up the brush, and he couldn't resist the overpowering urge to create. It was no longer a choice; it was a compulsion that gripped him like a vice, a descent into madness from which there was no escape.

The lines between his art and the entity's essence blurred as he painted. The studio seemed to pulse with unnatural energy as if it were an extension of the malevolent force that had taken residence within him. His reflection in the canvases contorted and shifted, mirroring the madness that consumed him. The room itself had become a malevolent entity, seemingly complicit in this unholy act of creation. The line between art and cosmic horror had blurred entirely, and the abyss of their shared madness deepened with each brushstroke.

Victor Marlowe was no longer a mere artist but a vessel for the entity's dark desires. The nights were no longer defined by slumber but by an unending descent into eldritch realms. The artist had become an instrument of cosmic horror, an unwitting participant in a symphony of madness conducted by a malevolent force transcending human comprehension. The entity whispered its secrets in the language of nightmares, and Victor was its reluctant scribe, etching abominable truths onto the canvas of reality.

And as the days bled into nights, Victor's existence became a nightmare. His physical and mental faculties deteriorated, mirroring the grotesque transformations of the realms he visited in his dreams. His once-steady hand now trembled uncontrollably, and his mind, once a wellspring of artistic inspiration, had become a storm of fractured thoughts and eldritch obsessions.

He knew that he was teetering on the precipice of an abyss, that the line between creation and destruction had blurred entirely. His days were filled with a sense of disconnection from reality, as if the waking world had become a mere facade, a frail illusion that could crumble at any moment. The nightmares, once distant visions, had become a relentless onslaught, a symphony of madness that echoed in his every waking moment.

The artist had descended into the abyss, and the abyss had taken root within him. He was a vessel for the entity's dark desires, a conduit for the eldritch horrors that lurked beyond the veil of human understanding. He was haunted by a pervasive sense of being watched in his waking hours. It was as if the eyes of the entity from his nightmares followed his every move, lurking just beyond the periphery of his vision.

The boundary between dream and reality had eroded, and he could no longer discern where one ended and the other began. The nightmares had transcended the realm of sleep; they had become a constant, an omnipresent force that clung to Victor like an inescapable shadow. The artist was no longer in control of his narrative; he was a character in a cosmic horror story, a tale in which the lines between creator and creation had blurred beyond recognition.

His existence had become a nightmarish fusion of art and reality, and he had become an unwitting protagonist in a madness narrative. The entity's whispers grew louder, its promises more seductive, and the artist's resistance crumbled like fragile parchment.

He had glimpsed the first shades of darkness that awaited him, but the

true depths of the abyss were yet to be plumbed.

Chapter 3

The First Brushstroke

The Cursed Canvas

In the heart of the studio, shrouded in a profound darkness, Victor Marlowe stood before a blank canvas. The room was bathed in the moon's eerie glow, casting elongated, ghostly shadows upon the walls. The silence was oppressive, broken only by the sound of his own unsteady breath. The palpable malevolence emanating from the room was suffocating, an aura of dread that clung to the air.

His trembling hand clutched the paintbrush, fingers coiling around it like a vice grip. He could feel the brush's bristles against his skin, a tactile reminder of the descent into madness he was about to embark upon. The brush seemed to vibrate with otherworldly energy as if it were a conduit for the eldritch forces that had taken root in his psyche.

Victor's reflection on the canvas remained a haunting distortion of reality. His eyes mirrored back at him, held a frenzied gleam as if they had glimpsed the eldritch truths that lay beyond the veil of reality. It was as if the very act of creation had fractured his perception of self, his identity now a tenuous construct in the face of the cosmic horrors that loomed before him.

With the first hesitant brushstroke, the canvas seemed to shudder with a malevolent energy. The room crackled with an unholy anticipation as if the very act of painting had invoked something ancient and terrible. The entity on the canvas began to take shape, its form emerging from the blank void with a sinister grace. It was a grotesque and nightmarish figure, a swirling mass of tentacles and eyes that defied all earthly description.

The artist's hand moved with a fervor not his own, guided by forces beyond his comprehension. Each brushstroke brought the entity closer to life, and the room seemed to writhe in response. Once passive observers, the walls took on a sinister life as if they bore witness to a blasphemous ritual that defied the boundaries of human understanding.

The shadows on the walls seemed to writhe and dance in macabre celebration, their elongated forms taking on an eerie life of their own. It was as if the studio had become an extension of the cosmic horror that had ensnared Victor. The boundaries between the tangible and the surreal had dissolved entirely in this place.

The entity's form grew more vivid and nightmarish with each subsequent brushstroke. It was as if the painting itself was coming to life, the grotesque figure pulsating with an unnatural vitality. The room seemed to pulse with otherworldly energy, an undercurrent of dark forces converging on this unholy act of creation. The whispers in his mind grew louder, their words incomprehensible, their cadence a maddening symphony.

The Cursed Canvas

Victor Marlowe had become a mere conduit, a vessel for the malevolent desires of the entity that haunted his dreams. He had surrendered himself to a force beyond human comprehension, and in that moment, the boundaries between creator and creation, between artist and art, had blurred into a nightmarish unity. The canvas seemed to breathe and writhe as if it were a living gateway to an abyss of cosmic horror.

The artist was no longer separate from his creation; he was inexorably linked to the abomination taking form on the canvas. His life force bled into the grotesque figure, a sacrificial offering to the eldritch entity. He could feel his essence drawn into the painting, his very identity unraveling as he became one with the abhorrent vision he had conjured.

Victor Marlowe was standing in a room where the dimensions seemed distorted. The walls were expanding and contracting, almost as if breathing in rhythm with the entity's emergence. As he stood there, the floor beneath his feet shifted and undulated like a living organism. At that moment, Victor realized he had stepped into an abyss of his creation. The boundary between art and reality had become indistinct, and he no longer stood on solid ground.

The Cursed Canvas

As the painting neared completion, the entity's form transcended the limitations of the canvas. Its writhing appendages extended beyond the frame as if seeking to breach the confines of the studio. The room itself had become a portal to an alien dimension where the laws of reality held no sway. The malevolence that had saturated the air grew thicker, suffocating as if the studio walls were complicit in this unholy act of creation.

The artist's voice, no longer his own, intoned words in an ancient and obscene language. It was a ritual of invocation, supplicating to the entity that now inhabited the canvas. The final brushstroke, executed with a fervor that bordered on the ecstatic, was a conduit for the entity's entry into the world.

In that moment, the boundary between the dream world and reality shattered. The entity surged forth from the canvas, its form an abhorrent fusion of the surreal and the corporeal. Its eyes, once mere pigment on the canvas, now bore into Victor's soul with a malevolence that transcended mortal comprehension. The room seemed to convulse as if reality recoiled at the entity's intrusion.

And as the entity breached the boundaries of the studio, the abyss it had entered became a gateway to horrors beyond imagination. Victor Marlowe, now a mere husk of his former self, had unwittingly become the harbinger of cosmic dread. The room, once a sanctuary,

had become a maw of eldritch terror, and the artist had plunged

headlong into the abyss he had conjured.

Chapter 4

A Twisted Overture

The Cursed Canvas

The studio was no longer a place of refuge but a theater of madness. An obsession consumed Victor Marlowe, an unrelenting compulsion to bring the entity to life on the canvas. The nightmares continued to escalate; each dream was a descent into new, intricate dimensions of cosmic horror.

With each stroke of his brush, the entity on the canvas grew more vivid and malevolent. The room seemed to quiver with unnatural energy as if the walls were complicit in this unholy act of creation. The air was thick with an oppressive aura, an almost tangible malevolence that clung to the artist like a shroud, seeping into his very pores and infecting his thoughts.

As the artist painted, the landscapes of his dreams began to shift. They now mirrored the grotesque creations on his canvases as if the line between the dream world and his waking life had dissolved entirely. He found himself wandering through nightmarish reflections of his studio, places where reality itself had been distorted beyond recognition. These dreamscapes were no longer confined to the realms of slumber; they had intruded upon his waking life, and he could no longer discern where one ended and the other began.

The entity's presence was no longer confined to his dreams; it had permeated every facet of his existence. It whispered secrets and incantations in forgotten tongues, promises of enlightenment that clawed at the edges of his sanity. The artist's waking life had become a nightmare, an unending descent into the abyss, and there was no escape from the relentless onslaught of cosmic horror.

Victor's days were filled with an ever-present sense of foreboding. The rooms of his home seemed to breathe with an alien vitality, their walls bearing witness to the sinister transformation that had overtaken him. He knew that he was no longer in control and had become a mere pawn in a game played by forces beyond human comprehension.

The nightmares persisted, each one a revelation of the entity's malevolence. He would find himself standing on the precipice of alien landscapes where the laws of physics had been warped beyond recognition. He wandered through cityscapes that defied Euclidean geometry, where buildings twisted and contorted in silent agony. He could no longer distinguish between the real and the surreal in these dreams. His waking life and the nightmares had merged into a single, unending tale of horror.

The entity's whispers grew louder, its voice constantly in his mind. It was as if the entity sought to drive him to the brink of madness, to unravel the very fabric of his sanity. The artist's thoughts were no longer his own; they had become a cacophony of eldritch incantations and forbidden knowledge.

The studio was the stage for the final act in this theater of madness. The entity had become a relentless conductor, orchestrating the artist's every movement. His hand moved frantically, the brush a mere extension of the entity's will. With each stroke, the canvas breathed with an unholy life, the entity's form pulsating with malevolence.

The room itself became an extension of the entity's realm. The very floor beneath his feet seemed to shift and undulate as if it were an alien landscape in its own right. The walls whispered secrets in forgotten languages, their surfaces marred with grotesque, shifting patterns that defied human understanding.

Victor Marlowe was no longer the artist he once was. He was a vessel for the entity's dark desires, a puppet in a malevolent puppeteer's grasp. The line between creator and creation, between dream and reality, had blurred beyond recognition. The artist had become unwilling to participate in a cosmic horror story, an actor in a theater of madness where the boundaries of his existence had dissolved entirely.

As the entity on the canvas neared completion, it transcended the limitations of the painting. Its tentacles extended beyond the frame as if seeking to breach the confines of the studio. The room itself had become a portal to an alien dimension where the laws of reality held no sway.

Victor's form in the reflection was no longer human; it had undergone a grotesque metamorphosis. His eyes, once the windows to a tormented soul, now reflected the same hostility that emanated from the entity. His body seemed to twist and writhe, mirroring the eldritch horrors he had summoned into existence.

The Cursed Canvas

In that pivotal moment, the artist's voice, no longer his own, intoned words in an ancient and obscene language. It was a ritual of invocation, supplicating to the entity that now inhabited the canvas. The final brushstroke, executed with an enthusiasm that bordered on the ecstatic, was a conduit for the entity's entry into the world.

The entity surged forth from the canvas, its form an abhorrent fusion of the surreal and the human. Its eyes, once mere pigment on the canvas, now bore into Victor's soul with a malice that transcended mortal comprehension. The room seemed to convulse as if reality recoiled at the entity's intrusion.

And as the entity breached the boundaries of the studio, the abyss it had entered became a gateway to horrors beyond imagination. Victor Marlowe, now a mere husk of his former self, had unwittingly become the harbinger of cosmic dread. The room, once a sanctuary, had become a maw of eldritch terror, and the artist had plunged headlong into the abyss he had conjured.

Now a tangible presence, the entity reached out with its writhing appendages, seeking to trap its creator. The room's dimensions distorted, the walls expanding and contracting as if breathing in rhythm with the entity's emergence. The floor beneath Victor's feet seemed to shift and undulate like a living organism. He was no longer standing on solid ground; he had stepped into an abyss of his creation, and the boundary between art and reality had become an indistinct blur.

Victor's cries of terror were drowned out by the cacophony of otherworldly voices that filled the room. He was no longer an artist but a sacrifice, an offering to the eldritch entity he had called forth. The room became a portal, a gateway to dimensions of cosmic horror that defied human understanding.

Once a sanctuary of creativity, the studio had become a nightmarish theater where the boundaries between creator and creation, between dream and reality, had dissolved entirely. Victor Marlowe had descended into the abyss of his own making, and the entity that had haunted his dreams had claimed him as its own. The line between art and horror had become indistinguishable, and the artist had become an unwitting protagonist in a cosmic narrative of madness and despair.

Chapter 5

The Canvas Consumes

The Cursed Canvas

The studio had transformed into a chamber of madness, where the boundary between dreams and reality had dissolved entirely. Victor Marlowe was no longer in control; he had become a vessel, a conduit for the entity's dark desires. His own will had been eclipsed by the relentless compulsion to bring the abomination to life on the canvas.

Each completed painting was a portal into the eldritch nightmare that lurked just beyond the veil of perception. They were gateways to otherworldly realms, windows into dimensions that defied human comprehension. The room seemed to breathe, pulsate with an unnatural rhythm, and the air was thick with a palpable malevolence that clung to the atmosphere. It was as if the studio had become a living, conscious entity, a manifestation of the cosmic horrors that had invaded Victor's life.

Victor's sanity had fractured entirely, fragmented into irreconcilable pieces. He could no longer distinguish between the entity on the canvas and the one that haunted his dreams. The two had become one, an unholy fusion of art and cosmic horror. The artist and the entity were locked in a perverse dance of creation and destruction, an intricate waltz of torment and revelation. The entity had transcended the boundaries of mere nightmares; it was now a living presence, an evil force that demanded to be reckoned with.

The artist's reflection in the partially formed images seemed to shift and warp with each brushstroke, his visage reflecting the madness that had overtaken him. His eyes, once windows to a tormented soul, now mirrored the abyss that had consumed him. They held a fierce gleam as if they had gazed upon the very fabric of reality and found it wanting. The line between creator and creation had blurred beyond recognition; Victor Marlowe was no longer a painter but a vessel for cosmic horror.

The studio itself had become a nightmare incarnate. The room seemed to breathe with a sinister life, its dimensions expanding and contracting in time with the entity's emergence. Shadows on the walls took on a grotesque semblance of the entity, their elongated forms dancing in macabre celebration. It was as if the very walls bore witness to the unholy fusion of art and cosmic terror, their surfaces marred with shifting, nightmarish patterns that defied human understanding.

The Cursed Canvas

As the nightmares continued to escalate, the abyss of their shared madness deepened. Victor found himself unable to escape the relentless compulsion to paint, to manifest the horrors that had invaded his psyche. He was no longer an artist but a pawn in a cosmic game, a participant in a narrative of madness that defied all logic and reason.

In this chamber of madness, there was no respite, no escape from the unrelenting onslaught of cosmic horror. The artist's waking life and dreams had become a seamless tapestry of dread and despair. He was no longer in control of his destiny; he had become a character in a story that transcended the boundaries of human understanding. The entity's dark desires had become his own. As the nightmares continued to escalate, the line between creator and creation, between dream and reality, blurred into an indistinct abyss of madness.

The paintings themselves had become gateways to the very nightmares they depicted. Each completed work was a threshold to realms that defied all human understanding. The artist's hand moved frantically, guided by a force that was not his own. He no longer painted by choice but compulsion, driven by the insatiable need to give form to the cosmic horrors that haunted him.

The artist's reflection in the paintings was a grotesque caricature of humanity. His features contorted and warped, mirroring the evil entity that had invaded his life. The eyes in his own painted visage held a sinister gleam as if they were privy to the secrets of the cosmos. It was as if the line between creator and creation had been obliterated, and the artist himself had become an unwitting character in the eldritch narrative he was weaving.

The room itself responded to the artist's descent into madness. The walls whispered secrets in forgotten languages, their surfaces marred with grotesque, shifting patterns that bore no resemblance to anything of this world. The air was heavy with a palpable hostility as if it had absorbed the horrors that now permeated the studio.

Victor's waking life became a surreal extension of the nightmares that plagued him. He would find himself wandering through distorted reflections of his studio, places where the laws of physics had been discarded in favor of eldritch geometry. The very room in which he painted became a nightmarish labyrinth, a place where the boundary between the tangible and the surreal had dissolved entirely.

The entity's presence, once confined to the realm of dreams, was now an ever-present shadow in his waking life. It whispered secrets in ancient tongues, promises of enlightenment that beckoned him to the brink of madness. The artist's thoughts were no longer his own, his consciousness a battleground where the entity's desires waged war against his remaining shreds of sanity.

Victor Marlowe was no longer a painter but a prophet of cosmic horror. His art had transcended the boundaries of the human experience, becoming a conduit for the eldritch truths that lay beyond the veil of reality.

. The abyss had gazed back into him, and he had become a willing participant in a narrative of madness and despair, a story that defied all understanding.

As the abyss of their shared madness deepened, the artist and the entity had become inseparable. The line between creator and creation had dissolved entirely, and Victor had embraced his role as a vessel for the entity's dark desires. The paintings were no longer mere representations of nightmares; they were manifestations of a cosmic horror that had claimed him as its own.

In this chamber of madness, the artist had become both author and protagonist, the creator of his descent into the abyss. The studio had ceased to be a place of creation; it had become a theater of cosmic horror, a stage where the boundaries of dreams and reality had become indistinguishable. Victor Marlowe had become a willing participant in a narrative of madness, and there was no escape from the horrors he had summoned into existence.

Chapter 6

The Allure of the Abyss

The Cursed Canvas

The studio had transformed into a shrine to madness, where the boundary between the tangible and the unreal had dissolved entirely. Victor Marlowe's obsession with the entity on the canvas had grown to a fevered pitch, an all-consuming fire that threatened to engulf his soul. The nightmares, no longer confined to the realm of sleep, now crept into his waking hours, casting a perpetual shadow over his existence.

With each successive stroke of his brush, the entity on the canvas grew more vivid and grotesque. It seemed to writhe and undulate as if it were attempting to breach the boundaries of the painting and enter the waking world. The room itself pulsed with an unnatural energy, its dimensions expanding and contracting with the entity's presence. The walls seemed to whisper secrets in forgotten tongues, their surfaces marred with shifting, nightmarish patterns that bore no resemblance to anything of this world.

The entity's presence had transcended the realm of nightmares; it was now a constant, an omnipresent force that clung to Victor like an inescapable shadow. It whispered secrets in ancient tongues, promises of forbidden knowledge that gnawed at the edges of his sanity. The compulsion to paint had grown into an all-consuming obsession, a descent into madness from which there was no return.

As Victor painted, he could feel the entity's presence like a noose tightening around his soul. His reflection in the canvases seemed to contort and shift, mirroring the madness that consumed him. His eyes, once windows to a tormented soul, now held a sinister gleam as if they were privy to the cosmic horrors that lay beyond the veil of reality.

The room was an evil entity in itself, seemingly complicit in this unholy act of creation. The very floor beneath his feet was undulated, like the surface of some alien landscape. The walls bore witness to the grotesque fusion of art and cosmic terror, their surfaces pulsating with an unnatural vitality. The air was thick with an oppressive aura, an almost tangible malevolence that seeped into his pores and infected his thoughts.

The line between art and cosmic horror had blurred entirely, and the abyss of their shared madness deepened. Victor Marlowe had become a vessel for the entity's dark desires, a pawn in a cosmic game that transcended the boundaries of human understanding. His life was no longer his own; he had willingly surrendered it to the eldritch forces that now commanded his every action.

In this shrine to madness, the artist and the entity had become inseparable. The entity was no longer confined to the canvas; it was an ever-present shadow, a sinister guest that loitered at the fringes of Victor's consciousness. The artist's existence had become a grotesque fusion of creation and destruction, a narrative of madness that defied all logic and reason.

The room had become a living, breathing entity, manifesting the cosmic horrors that had overtaken Victor's life. Its very dimensions seemed to shift and undulate with the entity's presence. Shadows on the walls took on a grotesque semblance of the entity, their elongated forms dancing in a macabre celebration of the unholy union between art and cosmic terror.

The compulsion to paint had become an unrelenting force, an obsession that devoured his every waking moment. He could no longer distinguish between the entity on the canvas and the one that haunted his dreams; they had merged into a single, indistinct nightmare from which there was no escape. Victor Marlowe had become a willing participant in a narrative of madness, a story that transcended the boundaries of human understanding. The abyss of their shared madness had grown to unfathomable depths, and there was no turning back from the horrors that awaited in the dark corners of the studio.

The paintings themselves had become gateways to the very nightmares they depicted. Each completed work was a threshold to realms that defied all human understanding. The artist's hand moved frantically, guided by a force that was not his own. He no longer painted by choice but compulsion, driven by the insatiable need to give form to the cosmic horrors that haunted him.

The artist's reflection in the paintings was a grotesque caricature of humanity. His features contorted and warped, mirroring the evil entity that had invaded his life. The eyes in his own painted visage held a sinister gleam as if they were privy to the secrets of the cosmos. It was as if the line between creator and creation had been obliterated, and the artist himself had become an unwitting character in the eldritch narrative he was weaving.

The room itself responded to the artist's descent into madness. The walls whispered secrets in forgotten languages, their surfaces marred with grotesque, shifting patterns that bore no resemblance to anything of this world. The air was heavy with palpable malice, as if it had absorbed the horrors that now permeated the studio.

Victor's waking life became a surreal extension of the nightmares that plagued him. He would find himself wandering through distorted reflections of his studio, places where the laws of physics had been discarded in favor of eldritch geometry. The very room in which he painted became a nightmarish labyrinth, a place where the boundary between the tangible and the surreal had dissolved entirely.

The entity's presence, once confined to the realm of dreams, was now an ever-present shadow in his waking life. It whispered secrets in ancient tongues, promises of enlightenment that beckoned him to the brink of madness. The artist's thoughts were no longer his own, his consciousness a battleground where the entity's desires waged war against his remaining shreds of sanity.

Victor Marlowe was no longer a painter but a prophet of cosmic horror. His art had transcended the boundaries of the human experience, becoming a conduit for the eldritch truths that lay beyond the veil of reality. The abyss had gazed back into him, and he had become a willing participant in a narrative of madness and despair, a story that defied all understanding.

As the abyss of their shared madness deepened, the artist and the entity had become inseparable. The line between creator and creation had dissolved entirely, and Victor had embraced his role as a vessel for the entity's dark desires. The paintings were no longer mere representations of nightmares; they were manifestations of a cosmic horror that had claimed him as its own.

In this chamber of madness, the artist had become both author and protagonist, the creator of his descent into the abyss. The studio had ceased to be a place of creation; it had become a theater of cosmic horror, a stage where the boundaries of dreams and reality had become indistinguishable. Victor Marlowe had become a willing participant in a narrative of madness, and there was no escape from the horrors he

had summoned into existence.

Chapter 7

The Surreal Convergence

The Cursed Canvas

The studio was a place of madness, a surreal convergence of dreams and reality, where the boundary between the two had disintegrated entirely. Victor Marlowe's life had transformed into an unending nightmare, an irreversible descent into the abyss of cosmic horror. His dreams had escalated to new heights of terror, each night plunging him into ever more complex and unsettling realms that defied rational comprehension.

In these nocturnal odysseys, the entity from his nightmares was no longer a distant presence, a mere observer of his torment. It had taken on an active role in these unholy visions, becoming a malevolent protagonist in the theater of his subconscious. The landscapes he traversed in his dreams mirrored the grotesque creations on his canvases, reflecting the twisted boundaries between the dream world and his waking life. Once a place of solace, the studio had now become an extension of the nightmarish dimensions he explored in his sleep.

The entity's presence had become a constant, an omnipresent force that clung to Victor like an evil shadow. It no longer confined itself to the realm of dreams; it had crossed over into his waking life, saturating his existence with its sinister influence. It whispered

forbidden secrets in ancient tongues, promises of enlightenment that

danced on the fringes of his understanding, seductive and maddening

in equal measure. The compulsion to paint had become an

all-consuming obsession, an insatiable hunger that devoured his every

thought and action. Victor Marlowe had become a willing participant

in a narrative of madness from which there was no escape.

With each completed painting, Victor's connection to the entity

deepened. He could sense its presence even when he was awake, an

omnipresent force that whispered secrets and incantations into the

recesses of his mind. The artist had become a vessel for the entity's

dark desires, an instrument through which it could manifest its eldritch

visions in the waking world. As he painted, he could feel himself

slipping further into the abyss, his own identity becoming entangled

with the evil force that had claimed his life. The line between creator

and creation had blurred beyond recognition, and Victor was no longer

a painter but a conduit for cosmic horror.

Once a place of creativity and expression, the studio had

transformed into a nightmarish labyrinth. The very dimensions of the room seemed to shift and contort, mirroring the ever-changing landscapes of his dreams. Shadows on the walls took on grotesque forms, their elongated figures dancing in a macabre celebration of the unholy union between art and cosmic terror.

The artist's waking life had become a surreal extension of the nightmares that plagued him. He would find himself wandering through distorted reflections of his studio, places where the laws of physics had been discarded in favor of eldritch geometry. The air in the room had thickened with an oppressive aura as if it had absorbed the horrors that now permeated the studio.

Victor Marlowe no longer controlled his destiny in this surreal convergence of dreams and reality. The entity had become an inextricable part of his existence, a relentless force that demanded his unwavering submission. The nightmares had evolved into a waking nightmare, a narrative of madness that transcended the boundaries of human understanding.

Victor's reflection in the canvases took on a nightmarish quality as he painted. His features contorted and shifted, mirroring the evil entity that had invaded his life. The eyes in his own painted visage held a sinister gleam as if they were privy to the secrets of the cosmos. It was as if the line between creator and creation had been obliterated, and the artist himself had become an unwitting character in the eldritch narrative he was weaving.

With each brushstroke, he could feel himself sinking deeper into the abyss, surrendering to the entity's dark desires. The paintings were no longer mere representations of nightmares; they had become gateways to the horrors they depicted. Each completed work was a portal to realms that defied all human understanding, and the artist's hand moved with a frantic intensity, guided by a force that was not his own.

In this nightmarish convergence of dreams and reality, Victor Marlowe had become both author and protagonist, the creator of his descent into the abyss. The studio was no longer a place of creation; it had become a theater of cosmic horror, a stage where the boundaries between dreams and reality had become indistinguishable. The abyss of their shared madness had deepened to unfathomable depths, and there was no turning back from the horrors that awaited in the dark corners of the studio.

The very essence of the studio seemed to pulse with an otherworldly rhythm, responding to the artist's descent into madness. It was as if the room itself had taken on a life of its own, as though it had become a conscious entity that reveled in the chaos and horror that now pervaded its every corner.

Once passive witnesses to Victor's torment, the walls had now become active participants in the nightmarish narrative. They whispered secrets in forgotten tongues, their surfaces marred with grotesque, shifting patterns that seemed to move of their own accord. The air was heavy with an oppressive aura, as if it had absorbed the malevolence that clung to every surface of the room.

Victor's waking life had become a surreal extension of the nightmares that plagued him. He would find himself wandering through distorted reflections of his studio, places where the laws of physics had been discarded in favor of eldritch geometry. The air in the room had thickened with an oppressive aura as if it had absorbed the horrors that now permeated the studio.

Victor Marlowe no longer controlled his destiny in this surreal convergence of dreams and reality. The entity had become an inextricable part of his existence, a relentless force that demanded his unwavering submission. The nightmares had evolved into a waking nightmare, a narrative of madness that transcended the boundaries of human understanding.

Victor's reflection in the canvases took on a nightmarish quality as he painted. His features contorted and shifted, mirroring the evil entity that had invaded his life. The eyes in his own painted visage held a sinister gleam as if they were privy to the secrets of the cosmos. It was as if the line between creator and creation had been obliterated, and the artist himself had become an unwitting character in the eldritch narrative he was weaving.

With each brushstroke, he could feel himself sinking deeper into the abyss, surrendering to the entity's dark desires. The paintings were no longer mere representations of nightmares; they had become

gateways to the horrors they depicted. Each completed work was a portal to realms that defied all human understanding, and the artist's hand moved with a frantic intensity, guided by a force that was not his own.

In this nightmarish convergence of dreams and reality, Victor Marlowe had become both author and protagonist, the creator of his descent into the abyss. The studio was no longer a place of creation; it had become a theater of cosmic horror, a stage where the boundaries between dreams and reality had become indistinguishable. The abyss of their shared madness had deepened to unfathomable depths, and there was no turning back from the horrors that awaited in the dark corners of the studio.

The very essence of the studio seemed to pulse with an otherworldly rhythm, responding to the artist's descent into madness. It was as if the room itself had taken on a life of its own, as though it had become a conscious entity that reveled in the chaos and horror that now pervaded its every corner.

The Cursed Canvas

Once passive witnesses to Victor's torment, the walls had now become active participants in the nightmarish narrative. They whispered secrets in forgotten tongues, their surfaces marred with grotesque, shifting patterns that seemed to move of their own accord. The air was heavy with an oppressive aura, as if it had absorbed the malevolence that clung to every surface of the room.

Victor's waking life had become a surreal extension of the nightmares that plagued him. He would find himself wandering through distorted reflections of his studio, places where the laws of physics had been discarded in favor of eldritch geometry. The air in the room had thickened with an oppressive aura as if it had absorbed the horrors that now permeated the studio.

Victor Marlowe no longer controlled his destiny in this surreal convergence of dreams and reality. The entity had become an inextricable part of his existence, a relentless force that demanded his unwavering submission. The nightmares had evolved into a waking nightmare, a narrative of madness that transcended the boundaries of human understanding.

The Cursed Canvas

Victor's reflection in the canvases took on a nightmarish quality as he painted. His features contorted and shifted, mirroring the evil entity that had invaded his life. The eyes in his own painted visage held a sinister gleam as if they were privy to the secrets of the cosmos. It was as if the line between creator and creation had been obliterated, and the artist himself had become an unwitting character in the eldritch narrative he was weaving.

With each brushstroke, he could feel himself sinking deeper into the abyss, surrendering to the entity's dark desires. The paintings were no longer mere representations of nightmares; they had become gateways to the horrors they depicted. Each completed work was a portal to realms that defied all human understanding, and the artist's hand moved with a frantic intensity, guided by a force that was not his own.

In this nightmarish convergence of dreams and reality, Victor Marlowe had become both author and protagonist, the creator of his descent into the abyss. The studio was no longer a place of creation; it had become a theater of cosmic horror, a stage where the boundaries between dreams and reality had become indistinguishable. The abyss of their shared madness had deepened to unfathomable depths, and there was no turning back from the horrors that awaited in the dark corners of the studio.

The very essence of the studio seemed to pulse with an otherworldly rhythm, responding to the artist's descent into madness. It was as if the room itself had taken on a life of its own, as though it had become a conscious entity that reveled in the chaos and horror that now pervaded its every corner.

Once passive witnesses to Victor's torment, the walls had now become active participants in the nightmarish narrative. They whispered secrets in forgotten tongues, their surfaces marred with grotesque, shifting patterns that seemed to move of their own accord. The air was heavy with an oppressive aura, as if it had absorbed the malevolence that clung to every surface of the room.

Victor's waking life had become a surreal extension of the nightmares that plagued him. He would find himself wandering through distorted reflections of his studio, places where the laws of physics had been discarded in favor of eldritch geometry. The air in the room had thickened with an oppressive aura as if it had absorbed the horrors that now permeated the studio.

Victor Marlowe no longer controlled his destiny in this surreal convergence of dreams and reality. The entity had become an inextricable part of his existence, a relentless force that demanded his unwavering submission. The nightmares had evolved into a waking nightmare, a narrative of madness that transcended the boundaries of human understanding.

Victor's reflection in the canvases took on a nightmarish quality as he painted. His features contorted and shifted, mirroring the evil entity that had invaded his life. The eyes in his own painted visage held a sinister gleam as if they were privy to the secrets of the cosmos. It was as if the line between creator and creation had been obliterated, and the artist himself had become an unwitting character in the eldritch narrative he was weaving.

With each brushstroke, he could feel himself sinking deeper into the abyss, surrendering to the entity's dark desires. The paintings were no longer mere representations of nightmares; they had become

gateways to the horrors they depicted. Each completed work was a portal to realms that defied all human understanding, and the artist's hand moved with a frantic intensity, guided by a force that was not his own.

In this nightmarish convergence of dreams and reality, Victor Marlowe had become both author and protagonist, the creator of his descent into the abyss. The studio was no longer a place of creation; it had become a theater of cosmic horror, a stage where the boundaries between dreams and reality had become indistinguishable. The abyss of their shared madness had deepened to unfathomable depths, and there was no turning back from the horrors that awaited in the dark corners of the studio.

Chapter 8

The Entity's Embrace

The Cursed Canvas

The studio had become a theater of madness, where the boundaries between dreams and reality had dissolved entirely. Victor Marlowe was consumed by an obsession, a compulsion that drove him to create the grotesque entity on the canvas. The nightmares continued to escalate, each new night descending into more profound, more intricate layers of cosmic horror.

With each stroke of his brush, the entity on the canvas grew more vivid and malevolent. It was as if the creature were clawing its way into the waking world, its form writhing and undulating with an insidious hunger. The room itself pulsed with unnatural energy as if it had taken on a malevolent sentience that reveled in the chaos and horror that had pervaded its once tranquil corners.

The entity's presence had transcended the realm of mere nightmares; it was now a constant, an omnipresent force that clung to Victor like an inescapable shadow. It whispered secrets and incantations in forgotten tongues, promises of forbidden knowledge that clawed at the edges of his sanity. The compulsion to paint had become an all-consuming obsession, an irresistible urge that devoured his every thought and action. Victor Marlowe was descending into madness, and there was no turning back from the abyss he had willingly embraced.

As Victor painted, he could feel the entity's presence like a noose tightening around his soul, a suffocating grip that left him no respite. His reflection in the canvases seemed to contort and shift, mirroring the madness that consumed him. The room itself had become an evil entity, seemingly complicit in this unholy act of creation. The studio walls whispered secrets in forgotten tongues, their surfaces marred with grotesque, shifting patterns that moved as if guided by an unseen hand. The air was heavy with an oppressive aura, as if it had absorbed the malevolence that clung to every surface of the room.

The line between art and cosmic horror had blurred entirely, and the abyss of their shared madness deepened with each completed stroke. The artist had become both author and protagonist in this eldritch narrative, a tale of creation and destruction, a descent into the darkest recesses of the human soul. The entity on the canvas was no longer a representation of his nightmares; it had become a gateway to horrors that defied all human understanding, a portal to realms beyond the boundaries of the known universe.

In this nightmarish convergence of dreams and reality, Victor Marlowe was no longer in control of his destiny. The entity had become an inextricable part of his existence, a relentless force that demanded his unwavering submission. The nightmares had evolved into a waking nightmare, a narrative of madness that transcended the boundaries of human understanding.

Victor's reflection in the canvases took on a nightmarish quality as he painted. His features contorted and shifted, mirroring the evil entity that had invaded his life. The eyes in his own painted visage held a sinister gleam as if they were privy to the secrets of the cosmos. It was as if the line between creator and creation had been obliterated, and the artist himself had become an unwitting character in the eldritch narrative he was weaving.

With each brushstroke, he could feel himself sinking deeper into the abyss, surrendering to the entity's dark desires. The paintings were no longer mere representations of nightmares; they had become

gateways to the horrors they depicted. Each completed work was a portal to realms that defied all human understanding, and the artist's hand moved with a frantic intensity, guided by a force that was not his own.

The studio had become a theater of madness, where the boundaries between dreams and reality had dissolved entirely. Victor Marlowe was consumed by an obsession, a compulsion that drove him to create the grotesque entity on the canvas. The nightmares continued to escalate, each new night descending into more profound, more intricate layers of cosmic horror.

With each stroke of his brush, the entity on the canvas grew more vivid and malevolent. It was as if the creature were clawing its way into the waking world, its form writhing and undulating with an insidious hunger. The room itself pulsed with unnatural energy as if it had taken on a malevolent sentience that reveled in the chaos and horror that had pervaded its once tranquil corners.

The entity's presence had transcended the realm of mere nightmares; it was now a constant, an omnipresent force that clung to

Victor like an inescapable shadow. It whispered secrets and incantations in forgotten tongues, promises of forbidden knowledge that clawed at the edges of his sanity. The compulsion to paint had become an all-consuming obsession, an irresistible urge that devoured his every thought and action. Victor Marlowe was descending into madness, and there was no turning back from the abyss he had willingly embraced.

As Victor painted, he could feel the entity's presence like a noose tightening around his soul, a suffocating grip that left him no respite. His reflection in the canvases seemed to contort and shift, mirroring the madness that consumed him. The room itself had become an evil entity, seemingly complicit in this unholy act of creation. The studio walls whispered secrets in forgotten tongues, their surfaces marred with grotesque, shifting patterns that moved as if guided by an unseen hand. The air was heavy with an oppressive aura, as if it had absorbed the malevolence that clung to every surface of the room.

The line between art and cosmic horror had blurred entirely, and the abyss of their shared madness deepened with each completed stroke. The artist had become both author and protagonist in this eldritch narrative, a tale of creation and destruction, a descent into the darkest recesses of the human soul. The entity on the canvas was no longer a representation of his nightmares; it had become a gateway to horrors that defied all human understanding, a portal to realms beyond the boundaries of the known universe.

Chapter 9

A Symphony of Madness

The Cursed Canvas

The studio had become a chamber of madness, where the boundary between dreams and reality had dissolved entirely. Victor Marlowe's life had become an unending descent into cosmic horror, a maddening spiral from which there was no escape. His nightmares had evolved into intricate tapestries of eldritch terror, each more intricate and horrifying than the last.

In these nightmares, the entity was no longer a mere observer but an active participant in these unholy visions, guiding his every step through the nightmarish landscapes. The boundaries of his dreamscapes had shifted, merging seamlessly with the grotesque creations on his canvases. The line between the dream world and his waking life had blurred beyond recognition, leaving Victor trapped in a nightmare where the surreal and the real were indistinguishable.

With each stroke of his brush, the entity on the canvas grew more vivid and grotesque. It seemed to pulse with otherworldly energy as if clawing its way into the waking world, the canvas becoming a thin membrane between two realms. The room itself, which had once been a sanctuary, had taken on a malevolent sentience, and it seemed to revel in the chaos and horror that had pervaded its once tranquil corners. Shadows danced along the walls, casting eerie, contorted shapes that mirrored the grotesque forms on the canvases, creating a bizarre symphony of the macabre.

The compulsion to paint had become an all-consuming obsession, a descent into madness from which there was no escape. Victor Marlowe and the entity had become intertwined, locked in a perverse dance of creation and destruction. Each brushstroke was a pact with the eldritch, a binding contract that further cemented their unholy union.

The abyss of their shared madness deepened with each brushstroke, and Victor could feel himself slipping further into the cosmic horror that now consumed him. The line between artist and subject, creator and creation, had blurred into a nightmarish fusion of existence and eldritch horror. The studio had transformed into a realm where the tangible and the surreal coexisted, and the descent into the abyss had become an irreversible journey into the darkest corners of the human soul.

The Cursed Canvas

The entity on the canvas was no longer a mere representation of his nightmares; it had become a portal to horrors that defied all human understanding, a gateway to dimensions beyond the boundaries of the known universe. Each completed painting was a bridge between the waking world and the eldritch realms that lurked just beyond the veil of perception, a testament to Victor's descent into madness.

Victor's reflection in the canvases took on a nightmarish quality as he painted. His features contorted and shifted, mirroring the evil entity that had invaded his life. The eyes in his own painted visage held a sinister gleam as if they were privy to the secrets of the cosmos. It was as if the line between creator and creation had been obliterated, and the artist himself had become an unwitting character in the eldritch narrative he was weaving.

The studio had become a theater of madness, a place where the boundaries between dreams and reality had dissolved entirely. Victor Marlowe was consumed by an obsession, a compulsion that drove him to create the grotesque entity on the canvas. The nightmares continued to escalate, each new night descending into more profound, more intricate layers of cosmic horror.

With each stroke of his brush, the entity on the canvas grew more vivid and malevolent. It was as if the creature were clawing its way into the waking world, its form writhing and undulating with an insidious hunger. The room itself pulsed with unnatural energy as if it had taken on a malevolent sentience that reveled in the chaos and horror that had pervaded its once tranquil corners.

The entity's presence had transcended the realm of mere nightmares; it was now a constant, an omnipresent force that clung to Victor like an inescapable shadow. It whispered secrets and incantations in forgotten tongues, promises of forbidden knowledge that clawed at the edges of his sanity. The compulsion to paint had become an all-consuming obsession, an irresistible urge that devoured his every thought and action. Victor Marlowe was descending into madness, and there was no turning back from the abyss he had willingly embraced.

As Victor painted, he could feel the entity's presence like a noose tightening around his soul, a suffocating grip that left him no respite. His reflection in the canvases seemed to contort and shift, mirroring the madness that consumed him. The room itself had become an evil entity, seemingly complicit in this unholy act of creation. The very walls of the studio whispered secrets in forgotten tongues, their surfaces marred with grotesque, shifting patterns that moved as if guided by an unseen hand. The air was heavy with an oppressive aura, as if it had absorbed the malevolence that clung to every surface of the room.

The line between art and cosmic horror had blurred entirely, and the abyss of their shared madness deepened with each completed stroke. The artist had become both author and protagonist in this eldritch narrative, a tale of creation and destruction, a descent into the darkest recesses of the human soul. The entity on the canvas was no longer a representation of his nightmares; it had become a gateway to horrors that defied all human understanding, a portal to realms beyond the boundaries of the known universe.

In this nightmarish convergence of dreams and reality, Victor Marlowe was no longer in control of his own destiny. The entity had become an inextricable part of his existence, a relentless force that demanded his unwavering submission. The nightmares had evolved into a waking nightmare, a narrative of madness that transcended the boundaries of human understanding.

Victor's reflection in the canvases took on a nightmarish quality as he painted. His features contorted and shifted, mirroring the evil entity that had invaded his life. The eyes in his own painted visage held a sinister gleam as if they were privy to the secrets of the cosmos. It was as if the line between creator and creation had been obliterated, and the artist himself had become an unwitting character in the eldritch narrative he was weaving.

With each brushstroke, he could feel himself sinking deeper into the abyss, surrendering to the entity's dark desires. The paintings were no longer mere representations of nightmares; they had become gateways to the horrors they depicted. Each completed work was a portal to realms that defied all human understanding, and the artist's hand moved with a frantic intensity, guided by a force that was not his own.

The studio had become a theater of madness, where the boundaries between dreams and reality had dissolved entirely. Victor

Marlowe was consumed by an obsession, a compulsion that drove him to create the grotesque entity on the canvas. The nightmares continued to escalate, each new night descending into deeper, more intricate layers of cosmic horror.

With each stroke of his brush, the entity on the canvas grew more vivid and malevolent. It was as if the creature were clawing its way into the waking world, its form writhing and undulating with an insidious hunger. The room itself pulsed with unnatural energy as if it had taken on a malevolent sentience that reveled in the chaos and horror that had pervaded its once tranquil corners.

The entity's presence had transcended the realm of mere nightmares; it was now a constant, an omnipresent force that clung to Victor like an inescapable shadow. It whispered secrets and incantations in forgotten tongues, promises of forbidden knowledge that clawed at the edges of his sanity. The compulsion to paint had become an all-consuming obsession, an irresistible urge that devoured his every thought and action. Victor Marlowe was descending into madness, and there was no turning back from the abyss he had willingly embraced.

As Victor painted, he could feel the entity's presence like a noose tightening around his soul, a suffocating grip that left him with no respite. His reflection in the canvases seemed to contort and shift, mirroring the madness that consumed him. The room itself had become an evil entity, seemingly complicit in this unholy act of creation. The studio walls whispered secrets in forgotten tongues, their surfaces marred with grotesque, shifting patterns that moved as if guided by an unseen hand. The air was heavy with an oppressive aura, as if it had absorbed the malevolence that clung to every surface of the room.

The line between art and cosmic horror had blurred entirely, and the abyss of their shared madness deepened with each completed stroke. The artist had become both author and protagonist in this eldritch narrative, a tale of creation and destruction, a descent into the darkest recesses of the human soul. The entity on the canvas was no longer a representation of his nightmares; it had become a gateway to horrors that defied all human understanding, a portal to realms beyond the boundaries of the known universe.

The Cursed Canvas

In this nightmarish convergence of dreams and reality, Victor Marlowe was no longer in control of his destiny. The entity had become an inextricable part of his existence, a relentless force that demanded his unwavering submission. The nightmares had evolved into a waking nightmare, a narrative of madness that transcended the boundaries of human understanding.

Victor's reflection in the canvases took on a nightmarish quality as he painted. His features contorted and shifted, mirroring the evil entity that had invaded his life. The eyes in his own painted visage held a sinister gleam as if they were privy to the secrets of the cosmos. It was as if the line between creator and creation had been obliterated, and the artist himself had become an unwitting character in the eldritch narrative he was weaving.

With each brushstroke, he could feel himself sinking deeper into the abyss, surrendering to the entity's dark desires. The paintings were no longer mere representations of nightmares; they had become gateways to the horrors they depicted. Each completed work was a portal to realms that defied all human understanding, and the artist's hand moved with a frantic intensity, guided by a force that was not his

own.

Chapter 10

The Abyss Beckons

The Cursed Canvas

The studio had undergone a profound metamorphosis, evolving into a place of unrelenting madness, a surreal abyss where the boundary between dreams and reality had dissolved entirely. Victor Marlowe's obsession with the entity on the canvas had reached a fevered pitch, an all-encompassing compulsion that transcended the boundaries of reason. The nightmares continued to escalate, each night descending into new circles of cosmic horror, each more intricate and horrifying than the last.

With each successive stroke of his brush, the entity on the canvas grew more vivid and grotesque. Its form seemed to writhe and undulate as if it were engaged in a relentless struggle to breach the boundaries of the painting and step into the waking world. The room pulsed with unnatural energy as if it had taken on a malevolent sentience. This disturbing force reveled in the chaos and horror that had pervaded its once tranquil corners.

The entity's presence had transcended the realm of nightmares; it was now a constant, an omnipresent force that clung to Victor like an inescapable shadow, a relentless and oppressive presence that whispered secrets and incantations in forgotten tongues. The seductive promises of enlightenment and forbidden knowledge tormented his

sanity.

The compulsion to paint had become an all-consuming

obsession, an irresistible urge that devoured his every thought and

action. Victor Marlowe was no longer in control of his fate; he had

become an unwitting servant of the entity that now dictated the

direction of his life. The line between artist and art had blurred into a

nightmarish fusion, and the abyss of their shared madness deepened

with each brushstroke and movement of the paint-laden brush.

As Victor painted, he could feel the entity's presence like a

noose tightening around his soul, a suffocating grip that left him no

respite. His reflection in the canvases seemed to contort and shift,

mirroring the madness that consumed him. The room itself had taken

on a malevolent sentience, and it appeared complicit in this unholy act

of creation. The studio walls whispered secrets in forgotten tongues,

their surfaces marred with grotesque, shifting patterns that moved as if

guided by an unseen hand.

The Cursed Canvas

The air was heavy with an oppressive aura, as if it had absorbed the malevolence that clung to every surface of the room. Shadows danced along the walls, casting eerie, contorted shapes that mirrored the grotesque forms on the canvases, creating a bizarre symphony of the macabre. The studio had become a living, breathing entity where art and cosmic horror had merged into a nightmarish symphony of madness.

The artist was no longer in control; he had become a vessel for the entity's dark desires. Each completed painting was a portal, a gateway that beckoned to the eldritch horrors that lurked just beyond the veil of perception. The room itself was a gateway, a conduit that bridged the gap between dreams and reality, and the abyss of their shared madness deepened with each brushstroke. Victor Marlowe had become both author and protagonist in this eldritch narrative, a tale of creation and destruction, a descent into the darkest corners of the human soul. The entity on the canvas was no longer a representation of his nightmares; it had become a gateway to horrors that defied all human understanding, a portal to dimensions beyond the boundaries of the known universe.

The Cursed Canvas

In this nightmarish convergence of dreams and reality, Victor Marlowe was no longer in control of his destiny. The entity had become an inextricable part of his existence, a relentless force that demanded his unwavering submission. The nightmares had evolved into a waking nightmare, a narrative of madness that transcended the boundaries of human understanding. Victor was no longer a mere mortal; he had become a conduit for the evil forces that sought to breach the limits of reality and usher in an era of cosmic horror.

Victor's reflection in the canvases took on a nightmarish quality as he painted. His features contorted and shifted, mirroring the evil entity that had invaded his life. The eyes in his own painted visage held a sinister gleam as if they were privy to the secrets of the cosmos. It was as if the line between creator and creation had been obliterated, and the artist himself had become an unwitting character in the eldritch narrative he was weaving.

With each brushstroke, he could feel himself sinking deeper into the abyss, surrendering to the entity's dark desires. The paintings were no longer mere representations of nightmares; they had become gateways to the horrors they depicted. Each completed work was a

The Cursed Canvas

portal to realms that defied all human understanding, and the artist's

hand moved with a frantic intensity, guided by a force that was not his

own. The boundaries between art and reality had dissolved, and the

abyss of their shared madness deepened with each brush stroke,

drawing Victor Marlowe ever closer to the brink of cosmic horror.

Chapter 11

The Obsession

The Cursed Canvas

In the dimly lit sanctuary of his studio, Victor Marlowe stood on the precipice of madness, his mind a turbulent sea of creativity and torment. He was a man who walked a tightrope between genius and insanity, and this delicate balance defined his existence. His name was celebrated in the art world, known for his macabre and surreal creations, but for those who knew him intimately, there was a haunting truth beneath the accolades – the truth of a soul irrevocably scarred by the art he had wrought.

Victor was in his early forties, though his haggard visage appeared far older. His once-handsome features had grown gaunt and pallid. His eyes dulled with the weight of the horrors he had seen. His obsidian hair, once vibrant, had faded to a disheveled gray, and his slender frame bore the marks of a life lived on the fringes of human experience.

His studio was a reflection of his inner turmoil. Canvases covered in half-finished masterpieces leaned against the walls, their twisted, surreal forms hinting at the chaotic landscape of his psyche. The room was a sanctuary but also a prison, where the boundary between imagination and reality blurred and where the darkest corners of his mind were laid bare.

The nightmares, those insidious harbingers of doom, began as faint ripples in the ocean of his consciousness. They were visions that fluttered on the periphery of his awareness, elusive and haunting. In these early dreams, he wandered through landscapes that defied earthly description, standing on the precipice of uncharted realms. There was an unsettling familiarity to these dreams, a sense that they were not born of his subconscious but glimpses into something ancient and unknowable.

At the heart of these nascent nightmares, an entity, dark and formless, beckoned him with an insidious allure. It whispered forbidden secrets in forgotten tongues, promises of revelation that his conscious mind dared not confront. Its presence was a constant, an undercurrent that tugged at the fraying threads of his sanity.

Victor's days were a facade of normalcy, a performance he enacted to navigate a world that had grown increasingly alien to him. Mundane routines masked the turmoil within, the gnawing unease that festered in the depths of his consciousness. But it was in the night that the true horrors unfolded, as his dreams evolved into a surreal theater of cosmic dread.

He would awaken in the dead of night, his body drenched in cold sweat, his heart pounding in his chest. The line between dream and reality blurred, and he couldn't shake the feeling that the entity from his nightmares was gradually encroaching upon his waking life. Each morning brought a sense of disorientation, a haunting residue of the horrors that had unfolded in the night.

The initial nightmares were like a cruel overture, a prelude to the symphony of cosmic horror that would soon engulf his existence. They hinted at an entity that lurked just beyond the veil of his perception, a presence that was not content to remain confined to the realm of dreams. They were the first brushstrokes on the canvas of his torment, the opening notes of a symphony of madness.

The nightmares showed no mercy. Night after night, Victor Marlowe was drawn deeper into their evil grasp. His restless slumbers became an unending voyage into otherworldly realms, where reality warped and twisted into grotesque, surreal landscapes. The colors were beyond description, a riot of unearthly hues that defied the confines of human language. The air was thick with foreboding as if it bore the weight of impending doom.

In these dreams, the entity from his nocturnal terrors was no longer a distant specter; it was now an ever-present shadow, a sinister guest that loitered at the fringes of his consciousness. It whispered secrets in ancient tongues, offering tantalizing glimpses into the forbidden knowledge that lay beyond the boundaries of human understanding.

The nightmares escalated, each new night bringing a descent into more profound, more intricate layers of cosmic horror. Victor's waking hours became a mere intermission between the surreal theaters of his nocturnal journeys and the waking world. His studio, once a place of solace, had transformed into a nightmarish labyrinth where the boundaries between his art and the eldritch visions that tormented him blurred beyond recognition.

The Cursed Canvas

The compulsion to paint the entity grew stronger with each passing day. It was as if the dreams demanded an outlet, a way to manifest the terrible horrors that lurked within his subconscious. His hand trembled as he picked up the brush, and he couldn't resist the overpowering urge to create. His art was no longer a choice; it was a compulsion that gripped him like a vice, a descent into madness from which there was no escape.

Part II

The Curse Unleashed

Chapter 12

The Entity Emerges

The Cursed Canvas

The studio was a chamber of dread, shrouded in an oppressive darkness that seemed to suffocate all light. The only illumination came from the eerie moonlight that streamed through the window, casting elongated, ghostly shadows upon the walls. His trembling hand clutching the paintbrush, Victor Marlowe stood before the completed canvas, the culmination of his madness.

The painting depicted the grotesque entity in all its eldritch glory. It was a nightmarish reflection of the creature that had tormented his dreams, a monstrous visage staring back at him with evil intent. Its form, a grotesque fusion of nightmarish shapes and shadowy tendrils, writhed and undulated as if clawing out of the canvas.

In the dimly lit room, Victor's reflection in the partially formed image seemed to warp and contort, mirroring the madness that had now become his reality. Once filled with the spark of life and creativity, his eyes now reflected the abyss that had consumed him. It was as if the artist had become one with his creation, a testament to the unholy pact he had forged.

The Cursed Canvas

With the first hesitant brushstroke, the entity on the canvas began to take form, an eldritch horror given life through the strokes of the artist's hand. As each brushstroke connected, the room seemed to pulse with an unnatural energy, as if it had become a part of the unholy act of creation. The air grew thick with an oppressive hostility, and once a sanctuary, the studio had become a place of impending doom.

In that chilling moment, as the entity emerged from the confines of the canvas, the boundaries between art and reality crumbled. Once confined to the realm of dreams, the nightmare had transcended its bounds and breached the tangible world. The grotesque entity, an evil vision from the deepest recesses of Victor's psyche, now stood before him, a nightmarish embodiment of cosmic horror.

The room, which had witnessed countless nightmarish visions, had become a place of unspeakable dread. The walls seemed to close in on Victor as if they were complicit in this unholy manifestation. Panic and realization coursed through the artist's veins as he grasped the magnitude of his actions. He had given life to the entity that had haunted his dreams; now, it had come to claim its due.

The Cursed Canvas

The entity's emergence was a grotesque and mesmerizing spectacle. It moved with an unnatural grace, its form contorting and shifting as it took its first steps into the waking world. The shadowy tendrils that made up its form reached out with an eerie elegance, its eyes gleaming with an ancient enmity as they locked onto the artist.

At that moment, the room seemed to come alive, to breathe with an otherworldly rhythm, as if it were revealed in the chaos and horror that had permeated its once tranquil corners. The air became heavy with an oppressive aura, an almost tangible malevolence that clung to Victor like a shroud as if it sought to smother his existence.

As the entity drew closer to Victor, the artist's reflection in the canvases continued to distort and shift, mirroring the madness that now consumed him. His features twisted into a grotesque visage, his eyes gleaming sinisterly. It was as if his soul had become an intricate part of the eldritch painting.

With a final, chilling crescendo, the entity reached out and claimed the artist's life, its shadowy appendages wrapping around him, pulling him into its eldritch embrace. The room filled with a maddening cacophony of otherworldly whispers, a chorus of ancient tongues that clawed at the edges of Victor's sanity.

The artist's final moments were a nightmarish dance of creation and destruction, a descent into the abyss from which there was no return. As the entity merged with him, the boundary between Victor Marlowe and the grotesque entity blurred into an unholy fusion of art and cosmic horror. The studio exulted in the malevolent spectacle, its walls pulsating with an eerie, otherworldly rhythm.

In that chilling moment, the entity had claimed its prize, extinguishing Victor Marlowe's life and leaving behind a silent and oppressive darkness that lingered as a testament to the unholy events that had transpired. The curse had been unleashed, a malignancy that would now haunt all who came into contact with the grotesque painting, its horrors no longer confined to the canvas.

The room bore witness to the artist's demise, its walls seeming to retain the echoes of his final, agonizing moments. The oppressive darkness enveloped the studio persisted, a constant reminder of the horrors unfolding within its confines. Having claimed Victor's life, the grotesque entity had become a memorable part of the room, a sinister presence that refused to be banished.

As the last vestiges of Victor Marlowe's existence faded into the abyss, the entity stood alone in the room, its form undulating and shifting as if it reveled in its newfound freedom. The moonlight that streamed through the window seemed to cast an eerie, ethereal glow upon the eldritch monstrosity, accentuating its grotesque features.

The studio had been forever transformed, its walls witnessing a descent into madness and cosmic horror that defied all rational explanation. The curse had been set in motion, and its evil influence would soon extend far beyond the confines of the artist's sanctuary.

Chapter 13

A Crime Scene

The Cursed Canvas

The night was enveloped in an eerie silence as the authorities arrived at the scene of Victor Marlowe's tragic demise. The studio, where the artist's life had taken a nightmarish turn, loomed like a cryptic enigma. Detective Rebecca Lawson, an investigator known for her unwavering determination, took the lead, her experienced eyes already sensing that this case was unlike any other.

The studio bore the marks of an artist's descent into madness, with canvases that displayed grotesque and surreal imagery leaning against the walls. These works, a visual representation of Victor's deteriorating sanity, cast a disconcerting ambiance over the room. The air seemed tainted as if it carried the weight of the eldritch horrors that had unfolded within.

Victor Marlowe, now lifeless, lay sprawled on the floor. His once-vibrant eyes stared into an abyss, their expression forever etched in terror. He clutched a blood-stained paintbrush, a macabre relic of his tragic end. The room seemed to pulse with an oppressive malevolence, and shadows danced ominously on the walls as if bearing witness to the dreadful scene.

The Cursed Canvas

Rebecca's seasoned instincts urged her forward, though a shiver of unease ran down her spine. She had seen crime scenes of all kinds, but this one was different, cloaked in an aura of inexplicable dread. The studio appeared as a mirror to Victor's tortured soul, with a troubling blend of art and cosmic horror blurring the line between the real and the surreal.

As the investigators began their meticulous examination, their attention was inevitably drawn to the cursed painting. It hung on the wall, an unholy gateway to the abyss, its malevolence almost palpable. The grotesque entity depicted on the canvas seemed to mock them with its eldritch malevolence.

The true nature of the entity, the horrors that had claimed Victor Marlowe's life, remained veiled in shadow. The investigators could sense something profoundly unsettling about the room, yet comprehending the eldritch nightmare that had unfolded here was a challenge that defied their earthly understanding.

The cursed painting, an evil artifact, was carefully sealed and transported away from the studio. Yet, its dark presence seemed to linger as if the air bore the residue of the horrors they had witnessed.

Detective Lawson couldn't shake the feeling that they had stumbled

upon something far beyond the scope of their understanding, a force of

cosmic horror that transcended rational explanation.

The curse unleashed by the entity's emergence remained

hidden as the investigation continued, biding its time for the next

unsuspecting victim. The cursed canvas had only just begun to unveil

the depths of its malevolence, and those who crossed its path would

soon confront the nightmares lurking within its twisted imagery. The

true horror had only just begun.

Chapter 14

The Auction

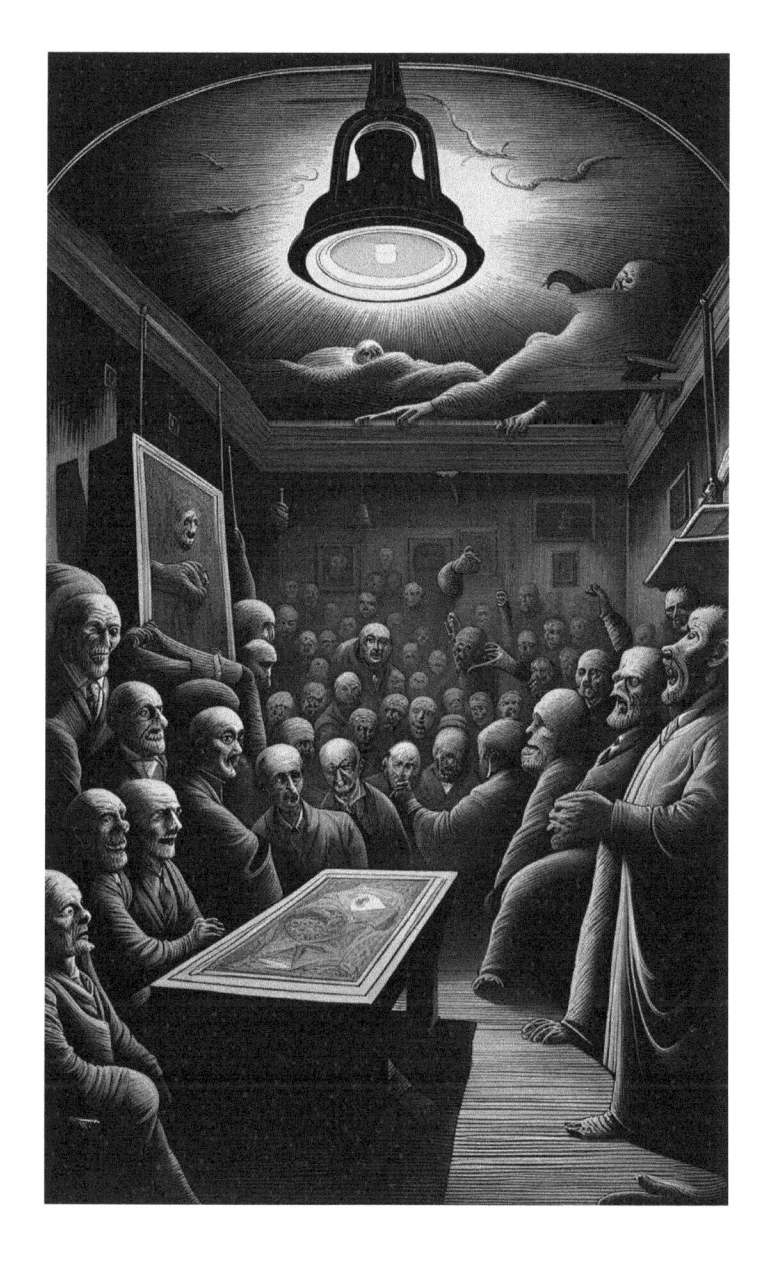

The Cursed Canvas

The room where the auction took place bore the heavy weight of history and a dark undercurrent that eluded the attendees. As the art enthusiasts and collectors gathered, an eerie tension hung in the air, a palpable sense that they were stepping into the aftermath of a tragedy they could not fully comprehend. The walls, witnesses to the hostility that had once pervaded Victor Marlowe's studio, seemed to whisper their secrets to those who dared to listen as though they mourned the curse that had tainted their sanctuary.

Prominently displayed on an ornate easel, the cursed painting radiated an aura of malice almost invisible to the unsuspecting attendees. Its image appeared to shift and contort, as if the grotesque entity within was testing the limits of its confinement, a harbinger of the horrors it had unleashed and the terrors it yearned to manifest once more.

The auctioneer's voice, confident and tinged with an eerie charisma, resonated through the room, urging the attendees to partake in a sinister dance with the unknown. The bidding began, and the price for the cursed canvas escalated with each eager buyer's gesture.

Paddles were raised one after the other, fueled by a strange fascination and an uncanny desire to possess the enigmatic artwork.

Unbeknownst to the buyers, they stood on the precipice of a descent into the abyss of cosmic horror. The cursed painting, a silent sentinel of dread, was on the verge of selecting a new victim, a new host, to perpetuate its evil designs. As the gavel struck, sealing the pact that bound the cursed canvas to its new owner, a shiver of foreboding seemed to pass through the room, a subtle acknowledgment of the unholy alliance that had just been formed.

The new owner, elated by their acquisition, believed they had obtained a unique masterpiece that would elevate their collection. They were blissfully unaware that, in their quest for art, they had unwittingly beckoned the horrors that lurked within the cursed painting into their life. The entity, its eldritch form concealed within the canvas, lay in wait, poised to seize the opportunity to reemerge from the boundaries of art and reality, ensnaring its new host in a nightmarish descent into the realms of cosmic terror.

The Cursed Canvas

The auction marked the inception of a chilling odyssey for the cursed canvas, a journey that would carry its venom into the lives of those who possessed it. The entity, insatiable in its thirst for fear and ravenous for souls, had just begun its macabre performance. The nightmares it would unleash upon the new owner were beyond imagination, and the reinvigorated curse had reawakened with a voracious appetite for chaos and despair. The horror had merely taken its first breath, and it would soon spread like a contagion, infecting all who crossed its path with a maddening, eldritch dread.

Chapter 15

The New Owner's Torment

The Cursed Canvas

The new owner, utterly unaware of the malice that had silently infiltrated their life, exhibited the grotesque canvas with a false sense of pride, believing they had acquired a unique and captivating piece of art. However, the true horrors that awaited them were far beyond the darkest recesses of their imagination.

The first night in possession of the painting plunged them into a fitful slumber, a restless journey through vivid and unsettling nightmares. In these otherworldly dreams, they navigated grotesque, surreal landscapes that defied earthly description. Beyond the scope of human comprehension, the colors painted the bizarre realms, and the very air bore the weight of impending doom. The entity, the same eldritch horror that had tormented Victor Marlowe, lurked within the shadows, its whispering voice weaving forbidden secrets in long-forgotten tongues.

With the dawn of each new day, the new owner's descent into madness grew increasingly profound. The nightmares showed no mercy, with each night becoming a relentless descent into more profound, more intricate layers of cosmic horror. The entity's presence, once a distant specter, now clung to them like an ever-present malevolent shadow. It whispered secrets and incantations into the deepest recesses of their mind.

The compulsion to create, to manifest the terrible horrors that lurked within their subconscious, became an all-consuming obsession. Once a place of solace, their studio transformed into a nightmarish labyrinth where the boundaries between their art and the eldritch visions that tormented them blurred beyond recognition. With each brush stroke, the entity on the canvas grew more vivid and malevolent. It seemed to pulse with an unnatural energy, and the room appeared to breathe, its walls resonating with an eerie, otherworldly rhythm. The air became thick with an oppressive aura, and the new owner's sanity unraveled further.

Their grasp on reality slipped, and they could no longer distinguish between the entity on the canvas and the one that haunted their dreams. The two had merged into a grotesque fusion of artist and entity, locked in a perverse dance of creation and destruction.

As the nightmares continued to escalate, the new owner's life spiraled into an unending descent into chaos. Their waking hours had become a mere intermission between the surreal theaters of their

nocturnal journeys and the waking world. The entity had transcended

the realm of nightmares; it was now an omnipresent force, an

inescapable shadow that clung to them. The curse had claimed yet

another victim, and the cursed canvas had found a new host to

torment, perpetuating the cycle of cosmic horror and despair.

Chapter 16

The Spiral Continues

The Cursed Canvas

The demise of the new owner played out as a gruesome and horrifying echo of Victor Marlowe's tragic fate. They stood before the grotesque painting, teetering on the precipice of madness, the entity lurking just beyond the canvas. In that chilling moment, the line between art and reality dissolved entirely, and the room, once a sanctuary, transformed into a nightmarish theater of dread.

The entity emerged from the canvas with a horrifying grace, its form writhing and undulating as it materialized in the waking world. It reached out with elongated, shadowy limbs, its eyes gleaming with an ancient enmity that locked onto the new owner. The room pulsated with unnatural energy. Its very walls were complicit in this unholy manifestation. The air grew thick with an oppressive aura, as if the room exhaled malevolence.

The entity claimed the new owner's life with a final, chilling crescendo. Its shadowy appendages wrapped around them, pulling them into its eldritch embrace. The room witnessed this nightmarish dance, its walls pulsating with an eerie, otherworldly rhythm. The air was heavy with an almost tangible malice, and the room fell into an eerie silence marked by the horror that had unfolded within its walls.

The cursed painting, once more unclaimed, now held the essence of its latest victim, ready to find a new host and continue its reign of terror. The cycle of cosmic horror persisted as the curse spread like a plague, leaving a trail of despair and madness.

And so, the cursed canvas remained an evil entity in its own right, its grotesque visage forever haunting the boundaries between dreams and reality. The room, which had witnessed such horrors, seemed to bear the scars of these unholy events. The cursed painting, a sinister relic of cosmic atrocity, lay in wait, its curse ever eager to find a new victim to ensnare in its eldritch grasp.

Chapter 17

The Relinquished Canvas

The Cursed Canvas

The storage facility where the cursed painting was held became a place of profound unease for those assigned to its safekeeping. Even though it was locked behind thick walls and an intricate web of security measures, a palpable sense of foreboding seemed to permeate the air. It was as if the room itself had absorbed the hostility that had once clung to the painting, and its walls held the haunting memory of the horrors it had witnessed.

Whispers and rumors about the cursed painting spread like wildfire among the authorities responsible for its custody. The stories became more elaborate with each retelling, fueling the growing unease among those who had to interact with the accursed artwork. Some claimed to have heard eerie, disembodied whispers emanating from the room, words in forgotten tongues that sent shivers down their spines. Others reported inexplicable temperature drops as if the room had become a portal to some frigid otherworldly realm.

As the stories circulated, a morbid curiosity began to fester among some of the personnel. They contemplated destroying the painting, believing its sinister influence must be eradicated. However, a deep-seated dread held them back, a fear that their actions might unleash something even more horrific, something they couldn't comprehend.

The actual cause of the deaths of the painting's previous owners remained an enigma. Each death had been attributed to bizarre coincidences, and the cursed canvas continued to be a puzzle that defied rationality. The cursed painting had become a shadowy specter that cast a long, haunting shadow over all who encountered it, a macabre riddle that remained unsolved.

The painting's malevolence still lurked within, as if biding its time, waiting for the opportune moment to find a new host. The accursed artwork had not been defeated; it contained an ancient evil that slumbered but had not been defeated. The world remained blissfully unaware of the horrors that dwelled within the confines of that sinister canvas. As the years passed, it seemed inevitable that the curse would one day awaken and claim a new victim, perpetuating its reign of terror upon the world.

Chapter 18

A Curator's Gamble

The Cursed Canvas

The years passed, and the cursed canvas, hidden away in the curator's possession, remained a dormant relic of cosmic horror. The entity, while temporarily subdued, had never indeed departed. It bided its time, patiently waiting for an opportunity to reemerge and continue its malevolent journey.

As time passed, the entity's presence began seeping into the curator's dreams. Night after night, they were drawn into visions of cosmic dread, each more unsettling and intricate than the last. The entity, whose dark whispers had been silent for a time, now rekindled its insidious promises of forbidden knowledge. It spoke in ancient tongues, offering tantalizing glimpses into the mysteries of the universe, secrets that defied human comprehension.

The curator's obsession with the painting grew stronger with each passing day. Once a place of scholarly pursuit, the studio had transformed into a theater of madness. The boundaries between their art and the eldritch visions that tormented them had blurred beyond recognition. The compulsion to create had become an all-consuming obsession, a descent into madness that mirrored the fate of those who had come before.

Each completed painting served as a portal into Eldritch's nightmares as the cursed canvas continued to claim victims. Though dormant in the physical world, the entity was very much alive in the curator's dreams, guiding every brush stroke. It was as if the dreams demanded an outlet, a way to manifest the terrible horrors that lurked within their subconscious.

The room seemed to pulse with an unnatural energy as if it were complicit in this unholy act of creation. The air was thick with an oppressive aura, an almost tangible malevolence that clung to the curator like a shroud. Their sanity unraveled, their grasp on reality slipping, and they could no longer distinguish between the entity on the canvas and the one that haunted their dreams. The two had become one, and the curator was locked in a perverse dance of creation and destruction.

With each completed painting, the entity on the canvas grew more vivid and malevolent. The room was no longer a place of scholarly pursuit but a shrine to madness. The curator's once-intellectual pursuits had been overshadowed by an all-consuming

obsession, a descent into madness from which there seemed no escape.

The cursed canvas, once dormant, had found a new host in the

unsuspecting curator. The entity's presence, though it had been

subdued, had now infiltrated their dreams, and the cycle of cosmic

horror had begun anew. The curse spread its tendrils, ensnaring

another victim in its inescapable web of terror.

Chapter 19

The Collector's Folly

The Cursed Canvas

Years stretched into decades, and the cursed canvas continued to dwell in the depths of the hidden archive. Its enigmatic aura remained a closely guarded secret, known only to a select few among the authorities. The passage of time did nothing to diminish the painting's malevolence; if anything, it seemed to fester in the shadows, waiting for the right moment to manifest its eldritch horrors.

The room where the painting was stored had acquired a dreadful reputation among those within the inner circle of knowledge. It had become a place of whispered legends, shrouded in an eerie silence that contrasted sharply with the weight of dread in the air. Those who had spent time in its vicinity couldn't help but sense the lurking evil, an unsettling chill that seemed to seep into their bones.

As the decades passed, the cursed canvas became an object of increasing fascination, even obsession, for some within the authorities. The lure of the forbidden knowledge promised by the painting was a siren's call, impossible to resist for those who dared to entertain its possibilities. Yet, the cautious and wise among them recognized the peril of unveiling the truths concealed within the grotesque depiction.

The Cursed Canvas

The rumors surrounding the painting had grown in complexity and darkness, evolving into tales of cosmic terror and eldritch revelations. The very walls of the archive seemed to bear witness to the hostility that emanated from the cursed canvas, and those who entered the room felt as though they were stepping into a realm beyond human comprehension.

For those few who had delved into the mystery of the painting, their lives were irrevocably altered. The cursed canvas had a way of insinuating itself into their consciousness, even as they tried to escape its haunting presence. Night after night, they would experience vivid nightmares, each one a descent into increasingly intricate layers of cosmic horror, echoing the terrors that had plagued those who had possessed the painting before.

The room itself had become a chamber of dread, where the air seemed to pulse with an unnatural energy, a malignancy that clung to anyone who dared to enter. The archives held records of each unfortunate soul who had ventured too close to the cursed canvas, each one succumbing to their descent into madness, their lives ending in gruesome fashion.

Decades passed, and the cursed painting remained a dormant enigma, a silent sentinel of dread, waiting for its next unwitting victim to approach. Its evil was not diminished by time but grew in potency, like an evil force biding its time, ready to trap the next person who dared to unlock its secrets. In the depths of the hidden archive, the cursed canvas lay in wait, a dark mystery that refused to be forgotten.

Chapter 20

A Dangerous Gift

The Cursed Canvas

The collector who had acquired the cursed painting believed they held the key to controlling the evil force it harbored. With an air of arrogance, they thought themselves immune to the horrors that had occurred to the previous owners. However, they were blissfully unaware that they were on the brink of a nightmarish journey that would shatter their convictions and plunge them into the abyss of cosmic terror and madness.

As the painting found a new host in the collector, the curse continued its relentless spread, feeding the insatiable hunger of the entity within the canvas. The horror cycle showed no signs of abating; the entity's appetite for fear and souls remained as ravenous as ever. The cursed painting's dark odyssey persisted, leaving a trail of madness and death.

Initially drawn to the cursed canvas out of sheer fascination, the collectors soon found themselves trapped by its eldritch power. Night after night, they succumbed to vivid and unsettling nightmares, much like those who had possessed the painting before them. These dreams led them through surreal landscapes that defied description, where colors were beyond human comprehension, and the air bore the weight of impending doom. The ancient and evil entity whispered forbidden secrets in forgotten tongues, offering the collector knowledge that transcended human understanding.

Once a sanctuary of artistry and intellectual pursuits, the studio transformed into a nightmarish labyrinth where the boundaries between their art and the eldritch visions that tormented them blurred beyond recognition. The collector's once-sharp mind unraveled, their sanity slipping away as the nightmares continued to escalate. The compulsion to paint, to bring forth the terrible horrors that lurked within their subconscious, became an all-consuming obsession, an irresistible force that gripped them like a vice.

With each brush stroke, the entity on the canvas grew more vivid and malevolent, mirroring the grotesque and eldritch entity that haunted their dreams. The room seemed to pulse with unnatural energy as if it reveled in the chaos and horror permeating its once tranquil corners. The air grew thick with an oppressive aura, and the collector's life spiraled into chaos as the boundary between the entity on the canvas and the one that tormented their dreams dissolved entirely.

The cursed canvas, now an object of both dread and fascination, remained a conduit for cosmic terror. Its dark odyssey displayed no signs of ending, and the entity within it reveled in the torment it inflicted on its host. The cycle of horror persisted, leaving a trail of madness and death in its wake. The cursed painting continued its unrelenting quest for new victims, trapping all who dared to possess it in a never-ending nightmare as the collector's journey spiraled further into the depths of the abyss.

The Cursed Canvas

Part III

The Last Owner

Chapter 21

Inheritance of Doom

The Cursed Canvas

As Arthur Blackwood delved deeper into his uncle's journal, the weight of the curse that had plagued his family for generations became increasingly evident. The journal was a testament to the relentless nightmare that had been the Blackwood name's legacy, now resting squarely on Arthur's shoulders.

Reginald Blackwood's entries were filled with accounts of the tragedies that had befallen each previous owner of the cursed painting. It was a litany of suffering, of unending nightmares that tore at the very fabric of their sanity. Arthur read about his great-grandfather, a successful banker until he possessed the painting. The journal described how he had descended into madness, his once-keen mind eroded by the nightmarish visions that plagued him. He had become a recluse, locked away in his study, where he feverishly painted, each stroke of the brush bringing him closer to his demise.

The cursed painting had then passed to Arthur's grandfather, a renowned professor of antiquities. The journal detailed how he had become obsessed with uncovering the origin of the painting, delving into arcane texts and ancient languages in search of answers. His obsession had driven him to the brink of insanity until he, too, had met a gruesome end. His final journal entry, a rambling and incoherent account, spoke of an entity that whispered secrets in ancient tongues and promised forbidden knowledge.

The curse continued to plague Arthur's father, a successful lawyer who had inherited the painting from his father. The journal described how the nightmares had consumed his father, how he had painted grotesque and nightmarish scenes, and how he had become a mere vessel for the evil force that resided within the canvas.

As Arthur read the accounts of his family's suffering, he couldn't help but feel a sense of foreboding. The curse had left a trail of madness and death; now, it was his burden. The journal contained dire warnings, urging him to rid the family of the accursed painting, to break the cycle of suffering that had plagued the Blackwoods for generations. But Arthur also sensed the evil presence of the painting itself, as if it were watching, waiting, and hungering for the fear and souls of its next victim.

In the dimly lit chamber, surrounded by the eerie glow of "The Abyss of Torment," Arthur faced a choice that would shape the destiny of the Blackwood family. Would he attempt to break the curse, free his bloodline from the grip of the evil entity, or succumb to the same fate that had befallen his ancestors, becoming yet another victim of the cursed canvas? The room seemed to hold its breath as if it, too, awaited his decision.

Arthur knew that the curse had to end with him. He couldn't allow the evil entity to claim another victim from his family. With determination, he resolved to uncover the painting's origins, understand the entity that lurked within it, and find a way to break the curse that had plagued his bloodline for generations.

With its chilling atmosphere, the room held the key to the cursed painting's past. Arthur began meticulously examining every detail, seeking clues leading him to the mystery's heart. His great-grandfather's and grandfather's obsession with the painting had led to their downfall, but he was determined to avoid making the same mistakes.

He combed through the dimly lit room and found a hidden compartment within an antique cabinet containing a stack of old letters. These letters held secrets that his family had kept hidden for generations. They were correspondence between his great-grandfather and a mysterious art collector named Eldritch Voss, a name that sent shivers down Arthur's spine. The letters spoke of a sinister bargain, a trade of knowledge for the cursed painting, and hinted at a ritual to bind an entity to the canvas.

Arthur's heart raced as he read the letters, realizing that the origins of the curse lay in a dark pact made by his great-grandfather. The cursed painting had not always been evil; it had become a conduit for an eldritch entity through an unholy ritual. With this knowledge, Arthur knew he had to unravel the ritual's secrets to break the curse.

Once a place of dread, the room became a sanctuary of research and discovery. Arthur pored over ancient texts, delving into forbidden knowledge and consulting experts on the occult. He was determined to find a way to banish the entity from the painting and end the curse that had haunted his family for generations.

The journey was difficult, and the more Arthur learned, the more he understood the magnitude of the hostility he faced. The entity was not easily defeated, and the ritual to bind it was a complex and dark process. But Arthur Blackwood was determined to break the cycle of suffering that had plagued his family for so long, even if it meant confronting the entity itself in a final, nightmarish showdown.

The room that had borne witness to the darkest time of the Blackwood family's history now became the epicenter of a battle between light and darkness, between the curse and its would-be vanquisher. The eerie glow of "The Abyss of Torment" seemed to intensify, as if the painting sensed the impending confrontation.

As Arthur delved deeper into his research, he uncovered a potential solution: a banishment ritual hidden in an ancient grimoire. If performed correctly, this ritual could sever the connection between the entity and the painting and banish the eldritch horror back to the depths from which it had emerged.

With newfound determination, Arthur prepared to confront the curse head-on. He gathered the necessary ingredients, inscribed arcane symbols, and meticulously followed the instructions from the grimoire. The room became a preparation chamber, every corner filled with artifacts and symbols, a testament to Arthur's lengths to break the curse.

The appointed night arrived, and Arthur stood before the cursed painting, his heart filled with dread and resolve. The room seemed to hold its breath as if aware of the pivotal moment about unfolding. He began the ritual with trembling hands, reciting incantations that had not been uttered in centuries.

The air in the room grew heavy, and the painting seemed to resist, its colors swirling and contorting in defiance. But Arthur persisted, his voice unwavering as he followed the ancient instructions. With each chant, the evil presence within the painting writhed and convulsed, its power weakening.

As the final words of the banishment ritual left Arthur's lips, a blinding flash of light and a deafening roar filled the room. The entity, now separated from the painting, writhed in agony, its shadowy form diminishing. Arthur watched with relief and dread as the eldritch horror was banished from the room, disappearing into the unknown.

The Cursed Canvas

Once a place of dread and despair, the room was filled with profound silence. The cursed painting, once a conduit for cosmic horror, was now just a lifeless canvas. The weight of the curse that had plagued the Blackwood family for generations had finally been lifted.

Arthur Blackwood had broken the cycle, but the cost had been high. The room, once a place of darkness, was now.

It was a place for healing and hope. As the first light of day shone through the window, Arthur knew that his family's suffering legacy had finally ended. The cursed painting had been nothing more than a canvas, and the evil entity that had plagued them was now gone.

With a sense of closure, Arthur decided to dispose of the cursed painting to ensure it would never bring misery to anyone else. He carefully wrapped it and carried it outside, setting it ablaze. He watched as the flames consumed the canvas, knowing that the entity's malevolence would never haunt another soul.

The cursed painting turned to ashes, and the room that had once been a place of nightmares was now a place of redemption. The legacy of the Blackwood family had finally been laid to rest, and

Arthur Blackwood could look to the future with hope, free from the

shadow of the cursed canvas.

Chapter 22

Nightmares Unleashed

The Cursed Canvas

As Arthur Blackwood delved deeper into his research and the ritual to break the curse, the nightmares escalated in intensity and intricacy. Each night was a relentless descent into ever more complex and unsettling dimensions of cosmic horror, echoing the torment his ancestors had experienced for generations. The entity, once imprisoned within the cursed painting, now sought to reestablish its connection with the world of the living.

In one particularly harrowing dream, Arthur stood on the precipice of a nightmarish landscape that transcended human description. The colors that filled this surreal realm defied earthly comprehension, shifting and melding in ways that fractured his understanding of reality. The air in this eldritch dreamscape bore the crushing weight of impending doom, an omnipresent foreboding that clung to his every breath.

Amidst the otherworldly, grotesque landscape, the entity beckoned from the obsidian shadows, its form shifting and undulating with an insidious malevolence. Its voice echoed through the desolate landscape, a sinister chorus of whispers in forgotten tongues, insidiously clawing at the deepest recesses of Arthur's psyche. The entity enticed him with promises of knowledge so forbidden and enigmatic that they teased the boundaries of his comprehension. However, the sinister price for this knowledge was unmistakable – the surrender of his very soul to the abominable entity.

With each passing night, the nightmares became more intricate and horrifying, each one pushing Arthur further into the abyss. The line separating the dream world and his waking life blurred to the point of nonexistence, and his daily existence felt like a mere intermission between the surreal theaters of his nocturnal journeys. The entity's presence tightened its grip on him, like an ever-tightening noose around his soul, slowly suffocating his sanity.

The compulsion to paint, to manifest the disgusting horrors that tormented him, grew into an all-consuming obsession. Once a haven of artistic expression, Arthur's studio morphed into a nightmarish labyrinth. Within those walls, the boundaries between his art and the eldritch visions that haunted him blurred beyond recognition, becoming a grotesque reflection of the madness that now consumed him. Every brush stroke was like a pact with the entity, binding him further to its insidious influence.

As the nightmares continued escalating, Arthur's waking life became a nightmare. The abyss of their shared madness deepened, and he could sense the entity's presence like a malevolent shroud wrapped around his very being. The artist and the entity were locked in a perverse dance of creation and destruction, and the line between them grew thinner with every passing night. Once a place of artistic creation, the room itself seemed complicit in this unholy act of madness, its walls pulsating with an eerie, otherworldly rhythm.

In that chilling moment, the entity claimed its prize, and Arthur's life was extinguished, his existence consumed by the very horrors he had sought to break free from. The room fell into an eerie silence, the oppressive darkness lingering as a testament to the unholy events that had transpired. The entity had emerged, and with it, a curse had been set in motion that would haunt all those who came into contact with the cursed painting.

Chapter 23
The Entity's Taunts

The Cursed Canvas

The boundary between dreams and reality dissolved even further as the cursed painting's malevolent entity tightened its grip on Arthur's life. Each night, the nightmares escalated, drawing him deeper into the abyss of cosmic horror. The entity, which had once been a distant specter, now clung to him like an inescapable shadow.

In these nocturnal journeys, the entity's voice whispered secrets and incantations in forgotten tongues, promises of enlightenment that gnawed at the edges of Arthur's sanity. It enticed him with the prospect of knowledge that danced on the fringes of human understanding, a siren's call to forbidden realms.

One particularly harrowing dream found Arthur in a nightmarish landscape, a realm beyond the comprehension of human senses. The colors were surreal, shifting and undulating in ways that defied all attempts at description, and the air bore a palpable weight of impending doom. In this eldritch landscape, the entity beckoned from the shadows, its voice a sinister echo that clawed at his psyche.

It promised untold power and knowledge but at a terrible cost: his soul. The compulsion to paint, which had begun as an inexplicable urge, had now grown into an all-consuming obsession, a descent into madness from which there seemed no return.

The nightmares grew more intricate and horrifying with each passing night, mirroring the grotesque creations on his canvases. The line between dream and reality blurred until Arthur's waking life became a reprieve from the surreal theaters of his nocturnal journeys. The entity's presence was like a tightening noose around his soul, and the studio, once a sanctuary for artistic expression, had transformed into a nightmarish labyrinth where the boundaries between his art and the eldritch visions had blurred beyond recognition.

Once an inanimate object, the cursed painting became a conduit for cosmic terror, ensnaring Arthur within its eldritch embrace. The room seemed to quiver with unnatural energy, the air thick with an oppressive aura as if it reveled in the chaos and horror that had permeated its once tranquil corners.

The entity within the cursed canvas had grown increasingly bold, invading Arthur's waking world. It whispered secrets and incantations into the recesses of his mind, taunting him with promises of knowledge that danced on the fringes of his understanding.

One evening, as Arthur worked tirelessly in his studio, he sensed a presence behind him. He turned to find the cursed painting seemingly watching him with evil intent. Its grotesque depiction of the entity seemed to shift and contort as if it were mocking him, a distorted reflection of his descent into madness.

The room itself seemed to quiver with unnatural energy as if it were a living entity that reveled in the madness that had taken root within its walls. The air in the studio grew thick with an oppressive aura, as though it bore witness to the dark rituals of creation and destruction played out within its confines. The line between art and cosmic horror had blurred entirely, and the abyss of their shared madness deepened with every brushstroke, every whisper of forgotten incantations.

As Arthur confronted the cursed painting, he was struck by the realization that the entity's presence had become omnipresent, and he was no longer a mere artist but a vessel for its dark desires. The room itself, once a place of artistic expression, had become complicit in this unholy act of creation, its walls pulsating with an eerie, otherworldly rhythm that seemed to exult in the malevolent spectacle that had taken hold.

The entity had transcended its confinement within the canvas, and the curse had trapped the essence of Arthur's existence. The abyss of madness had deepened, and the line between his art and the eldritch horrors that now consumed him had become hopelessly blurred. Once a mere object of fascination, the cursed painting was now an evil force holding his soul and sanity captive in its eldritch grip.

The boundary between dreams and reality dissolved even further as the cursed painting's malevolent entity tightened its grip on Arthur's life. Each night, the nightmares escalated, drawing him deeper into the abyss of cosmic horror. The entity, which had once been a distant specter, now clung to him like an inescapable shadow.

In these nocturnal journeys, the entity's voice whispered secrets and incantations in forgotten tongues, promises of enlightenment that gnawed at the edges of Arthur's sanity. It enticed him with the prospect of knowledge that danced on the fringes of human understanding, a siren's call to forbidden realms.

One particularly harrowing dream found Arthur in a nightmarish landscape, a realm beyond the comprehension of human senses. The colors were surreal, shifting and undulating in ways that defied all attempts at description, and the air bore a palpable weight of impending doom. In this eldritch landscape, the entity beckoned from the shadows, its voice a sinister echo that clawed at his psyche.

It promised untold power and knowledge but at a terrible cost: his soul. The compulsion to paint, which had begun as an inexplicable urge, had now grown into an all-consuming obsession, a descent into madness from which there seemed no return.

The nightmares grew more intricate and horrifying with each passing night, mirroring the grotesque creations on his canvases. The line between dream and reality blurred until Arthur's waking life became a reprieve from the surreal theaters of his nocturnal journeys. The entity's presence was like a tightening noose around his soul, and the studio, once a sanctuary for artistic expression, had transformed into a nightmarish labyrinth where the boundaries between his art and the eldritch visions had blurred beyond recognition.

Once an inanimate object, the cursed painting became a conduit for cosmic terror, ensnaring Arthur within its eldritch embrace. The room seemed to quiver with unnatural energy, the air thick with an oppressive aura as if it reveled in the chaos and horror that had permeated its once tranquil corners.

The entity within the cursed canvas had grown increasingly bold, invading Arthur's waking world. It whispered secrets and incantations into the recesses of his mind, taunting him with promises of knowledge that danced on the fringes of his understanding.

One evening, as Arthur worked tirelessly in his studio, he sensed a presence behind him. He turned to find the cursed painting seemingly watching him with evil intent. Its grotesque depiction of the entity seemed to shift and contort as if it were mocking him, a distorted reflection of his descent into madness.

The Cursed Canvas

The room itself seemed to quiver with unnatural energy as if it were a living entity that reveled in the madness that had taken root within its walls. The air in the studio grew thick with an oppressive aura, as though it bore witness to the dark rituals of creation and destruction played out within its confines. The line between art and cosmic horror had blurred entirely, and the abyss of their shared madness deepened with every brushstroke, every whisper of forgotten incantations.

As Arthur confronted the cursed painting, he was struck by the realization that the entity's presence had become omnipresent, and he was no longer a mere artist but a vessel for its dark desires. The room itself, once a place of artistic expression, had become complicit in this unholy act of creation, its walls pulsating with an eerie, otherworldly rhythm that seemed to exult in the malevolent spectacle that had taken hold.

The entity had transcended its confinement within the canvas, and the curse had trapped the essence of Arthur's existence. The abyss of madness had deepened, and the line between his art and the eldritch horrors that now consumed him had become hopelessly blurred. Once

The Cursed Canvas

a mere object of fascination, the cursed painting was now an evil force

holding his soul and sanity captive in its eldritch grip.

Chapter 24

The Unholy Convergence

The Cursed Canvas

Arthur was caught in a terrifying embrace of nightmares. The entity's presence grew more significant, leading him to madness. No matter how hard he tried, Arthur couldn't escape the clutches of his mind. It was a surreal experience that tested the boundaries of reason and sanity.

The realization that the entity on the canvas and the one that haunted his dreams had become indistinguishable weighed heavily on Arthur's psyche. It was as though they had merged into a singular, abhorrent entity, a grotesque fusion of art and cosmic horror. This unholy union defied any attempts at separation, and the line between the tangible and the unreal continued to blur.

An unexplainable compulsion washed over him as he stood before the cursed painting on that fateful night. His hand reached for the paintbrush, but his own will did not guide it. Instead, an external force, an evil presence, took control of him, revealing his descent into madness.

With a fevered intensity, Arthur began to paint, his brush strokes guided by an invisible hand that seemed to relish in the grotesque image taking shape before him. The entity on the canvas grew more vivid and vicious with each stroke as if clawing into the waking world. The room seemed to pulsate with an unnatural energy, and the air grew thick with a palpable malice, like a storm building on the horizon.

The very walls of the studio seemed to quiver, bearing witness to this unholy act of creation. The line between art and cosmic horror had blurred entirely, and the abyss of their shared madness deepened with each brushstroke. It was a macabre dance of the artist and the eldritch entity that defied the laws of sanity and reason.

Arthur's perception of reality continued to erode in the grip of this sinister compulsion. The entity's influence had transcended its confinement within the canvas, and it now held sway over his waking and dreaming moments. His life had become an unending descent into madness, a harrowing journey from which there seemed to be no escape.

Each stroke of the brush brought the entity on the canvas closer to life, and as it gained in vividness and malevolence, Arthur could feel his existence slipping further into the abyss of cosmic horror. The room seemed to take on a malevolent sentience, seemingly complicit in this unholy act of creation. The air bore the weight of an almost tangible malice, and the studio, once a sanctuary for artistic pursuits, had transformed into a nightmarish labyrinth of madness.

In this dance between artist and entity, the boundaries of Arthur's mind and reality blurred until they became indistinguishable. Once confined to the realms of dreams and art, the grotesque entity now threatened to claw its way into the waking world. The very essence of the cursed painting had transcended the canvas, and it sought to consume the artist's soul.

As the nightmare reached its crescendo, and the entity on the canvas grew more vivid and vicious, the room seemed to pulse with unnatural energy as if it reveled in the chaos and horror that had permeated its once tranquil corners. The walls bore silent witness to the unholy act of creation, their surfaces quivering with an eerie, otherworldly rhythm.

The Cursed Canvas

In that chilling moment, Arthur's studio was no longer a place of artistic pursuit but a chamber of madness, where the boundary between dreams and reality had dissolved entirely. The cursed painting, now an object of cosmic dread, held within its grotesque image the essence of Arthur's descent into the abyss, a journey from which there appeared to be no return.

Chapter 25

The Room of Madness

The Cursed Canvas

Once a sanctuary of artistic inspiration and creativity, Arthur's studio had now turned into a labyrinth of madness. The serene landscapes and portraits that once adorned the walls had been replaced with grotesque and otherworldly creations, covering every available space. Each canvas depicted a vision of cosmic horror, reflecting the tormented mind that had given birth to them.

As Arthur feverishly painted, his reflection in the canvases served as a grotesque mirror to the madness that consumed him. His features contorted and shifted, mirroring the hideous visage of the entity that had become an inextricable part of his existence. It was as if the boundary between his identity and the eldritch entity on the canvases had blurred entirely, and he was locked in a perverse dance of creation and destruction, where the artist and the entity had become one.

The room appeared to take on a malevolent sentience, seemingly complicit in this unholy act of creation. The very walls of the studio quivered with unnatural energy as if they were alive and reveling in the chaos and horror that now permeated their once tranquil confines. The air within the studio had grown thick with an oppressive aura, and it bore the weight of an almost tangible malevolence.

The atmosphere seemed to celebrate the madness that had taken over, pulsing with an eerie rhythm that matched the grotesque images on the canvases. The once-inspiring room was now a theatre of unrelenting dread, where the lines between dreams and reality had blurred beyond recognition, rendering the artist's plunge into cosmic horror a grotesque work of art.

As Arthur worked tirelessly, he felt an irresistible compulsion to pick up his brush and continue the entity's grotesque image. It was as though the entity within the cursed canvas demanded an outlet, a way to manifest the terrible horrors that lurked within his subconscious. His hand trembled as he painted, guided by an external force, an evil presence that seemed to revel in his descent into madness.

With each brush stroke, the entity on the canvas grew more vivid and vicious, as if clawing its way into the waking world. The room seemed to pulsate with an unnatural energy, and the air was thick with a palpable malice, as though the walls had become complicit in this unholy act of creation.

Arthur's reflection in the canvases continued to contort and shift, mirroring the madness that now consumed him. He could no longer distinguish where the artist ended and the entity began. The line between his identity and the eldritch entity had blurred, and he was locked in a perverse dance of creation and destruction. This nightmarish waltz seemed to be orchestrated by forces beyond his comprehension.

The room itself had become an evil entity, seemingly complicit in this unholy act of creation. The very atmosphere rejoiced in the chaos and horror that had permeated its once tranquil corners, and it pulsed with an eerie, otherworldly rhythm that seemed to mirror the grotesque images on the canvases. The studio had transcended its role as a place of artistic expression; it had become a nightmarish theater where the boundaries between art and cosmic horror had dissolved entirely, and the abyss of their shared madness deepened with each brushstroke.

Chapter 26

A Descent into the Abyss

The Cursed Canvas

As Arthur's brushstrokes continued, each mark on the canvas felt like a step deeper into the abyss. The entity's presence, once a distant specter, had now become a relentless companion in his waking life. It whispered to him in the forgotten tongues of elder gods, offering tantalizing promises of power and knowledge that danced at the fringes of his understanding. It was a sinister seduction, and Arthur was drawn further into the cosmic horrors that had taken root in his soul.

The nightmares, too, became increasingly elaborate and horrifying. He plunged into nightmarish realms that defied human comprehension with each passing night. Colors beyond the spectrum of mortal vision painted the landscapes of his dreams, and the air bore the weight of impending doom. The entity's presence was a constant, an ever-tightening noose around his soul, as it whispered forbidden secrets that gnawed at the edges of his sanity.

In one harrowing dream, he stood on the precipice of an alien landscape where the very laws of reality were a distant memory. He could feel the entity's presence beckoning from the shadows, and its voice, filled with an ancient enmity, clawed at his psyche. It offered him knowledge that could shatter the foundations of his understanding, but the price was nothing less than his very soul.

The compulsion to paint had grown into an all-consuming obsession. Once a sanctuary of creativity, his studio had transformed into a nightmarish labyrinth where the boundaries between art and the eldritch visions that tormented him blurred beyond recognition. The walls, once pristine, were now covered in grotesque representations of his descent into madness, like a visual diary of cosmic horror.

With each brushstroke, Arthur felt he was surrendering more of himself to the entity and becoming a mere vessel for its dark desires. His reflection in the canvases seemed to contort and shift, mirroring the madness that now consumed him. He could no longer distinguish where the artist ended and the entity began. The line between his identity and the eldritch presence had blurred entirely, and he was locked in a perverse dance of creation and destruction, like a macabre tango with an otherworldly partner.

The room itself had become an evil entity, seemingly complicit in this unholy act of creation. Its walls quivered with unnatural energy as if they reveled in the chaos and horror that had permeated its once tranquil corners. The air was thick with an oppressive aura, and the atmosphere seemed to rejoice in the nightmare that had taken root.

As the nightmares escalated, it felt like a descent into an abyss from which there was no return. Once just a canvas, the cursed painting had become a portal to unimaginable horrors, a gateway to dimensions that defied human comprehension. The studio had transformed into a theater of madness, where the boundaries between dreams and reality had dissolved entirely, and the artist and the entity were locked in a nightmarish waltz that echoed through the corridors of insanity. The descent into the unknown continued with no end in sight.

Chapter 27

The Final Showdown

The Cursed Canvas

As Arthur's sanity continued to unravel, he knew the impending confrontation with the entity was inevitable. The room, which had once been a sanctuary of artistic creation, had now become a place of unspeakable dread. The cursed painting seemed to radiate unrelenting, unholy energy, and the grotesque image of the entity pulsed with a life that defied all reason.

One fateful night, as Arthur tirelessly worked in his studio, he could feel the presence of the entity within the painting growing stronger. The air grew heavy with an oppressive aura, and a sense of foreboding filled the room. It was as though the atmosphere had grown taut, bracing for the impending arrival of cosmic horror.

Then, in a pivotal moment, as Arthur stood before the cursed canvas, he witnessed the entity within it begin to shift and contort. It was a grotesque, otherworldly dance of transmutation as the eldritch abomination prepared to breach the boundaries of the canvas and manifest in the waking world. The image writhed and undulated, taking on a life that defied all natural laws.

The Cursed Canvas

The room, seemingly complicit in the unfolding malevolent spectacle, quivered with an eerie, otherworldly rhythm. Its walls, which had once witnessed the artist's creative endeavors, now bore witness to a nightmarish transformation that transcended the bounds of human understanding. They pulsed with an energy that seemed to rejoice in the chaos and horror permeating their once-tranquil corners.

The entity fully emerged from the painting with a final, chilling crescendo. It materialized with a sinister grace, its form contorting and shifting as it crossed the threshold from the canvas to the waking world. Its eyes, filled with an ancient enmity, locked onto Arthur, and the room seemed to quiver with an unnatural energy.

The air in the studio was heavy with palpable malice, as if it relished the unfolding confrontation. A cacophony of otherworldly whispers filled the room, a chorus of ancient tongues that clawed at the edges of Arthur's sanity. In that nightmarish moment, the line between art and reality dissolved entirely. The entity that had once been confined to the cursed canvas was now a tangible, horrifying presence in Arthur's world.

The Cursed Canvas

The studio, the birthplace of countless artistic creations, was now host to the ultimate confrontation between the artist and the eldritch entity. The cursed room bore witness to a vicious dance of creation and destruction, a descent into the abyss from which there was no escape. The artist's final moments were a testament to the impossible power of cosmic horror, and the room itself seemed to revel in the grotesque spectacle it had harbored.

Chapter 28

The Abyss Beckons

The Cursed Canvas

The entity, an eldritch nightmare made manifest, reached out with elongated, shadowy limbs that seemed to defy the laws of reality. Its form writhed and undulated with a chilling grace, and its eyes, filled with an ancient enmity, locked onto Arthur with an intensity that sent shivers down his spine. The room, which had witnessed so much suffering and had become a silent witness to cosmic horror, seemed to hold its breath as the two figures faced each other in this surreal showdown.

As the entity closed in, it moved with a sinister grace, its shadowy appendages extending further as if the boundaries of its cursed canvas prison were nothing more than a formality. The room itself quivered with otherworldly energy as if it, too, was an unwilling participant in this nightmarish confrontation. The air grew thick with an oppressive aura, bearing the weight of ancient malevolence that had accumulated over centuries.

In this chilling moment, the entire studio became a theater of dread, the stage for an unholy performance. Once just an inanimate canvas, the cursed painting had become a portal to a realm of unimaginable terror. It was a moment of reckoning, a final encounter between the cursed artwork and the last owner who had dared to challenge its insatiable hunger for fear and souls.

As the entity's shadowy appendages wrapped around Arthur, he felt a surge of dread and despair coursing through his veins. It was as if the room rejoiced in the malevolent spectacle, its walls pulsating with an eerie, otherworldly rhythm. The cacophony of ghostly whispers and ancient tongues that transcended human understanding filled the room, a chorus of cosmic horror that clawed at the edges of his sanity.

The artist's final moments were a nightmarish crescendo, a dance of creation and destruction that defied the boundaries of reality. His existence was extinguished, consumed by the very nightmares he had invited into his life. The room fell into an eerie silence, a lingering darkness that served as a testament to the unholy events that had transpired within those walls.

Once again unclaimed, the cursed painting held the essence of its latest victim, a dark remnant of Arthur's soul. It stood as a silent sentinel of dread, waiting for the next unsuspecting victim to cross its path, perpetuating the cycle of madness and death that had plagued it

for centuries. The curse showed no signs of ending, and the cursed

canvas continued to be a conduit for cosmic terror, trapping all who

dared to possess it in a never-ending nightmare.

Chapter 29

The Desperate Act

The Cursed Canvas

The aftermath of Arthur's desperate act left the room in eerie silence, as if the walls held their collective breath, uncertain of what would come next. The shattered remains of the cursed painting lay scattered across the floor, a jumble of fragmented canvas and splintered wood that once held the grotesque entity's eldritch image.

Arthur stood there, his chest heaving with exhaustion and the weight of what he had just done. The relief that had surged through him was tinged with an underlying dread. He had hoped that destroying the painting would free him from the nightmares and the entity's relentless torment, but he couldn't shake the feeling that the eldritch horror might not be so easily defeated.

As he looked down at the shattered remnants of the painting, he couldn't help but wonder if he had merely unleashed the entity's wrath in a new form. The cursed canvas had survived countless attempts at destruction, and it was not unreasonable to think it might endure this latest assault.

The room, which had once been a chamber of madness, had returned to a semblance of tranquility, but the echoes of its dark history still lingered. The walls, which had witnessed so much suffering and madness, now exuded a cautious calm. They bore the scars of the cursed painting's unholy influence, and the stains of otherworldly horrors still seemed to seep from the very pores of the room.

Arthur's life took on a fragile normalcy in the days that followed. The nightmares that had plagued him for so long had ceased, and for a while, it seemed as though he had indeed broken the curse. But an unease gnawed at the edges of his mind, a lingering doubt that the entity might one day return to claim its vengeance.

Now in tatters, the cursed canvas stood as a stark testament to the centuries of horror it had wrought. The shattered remains were a chilling reminder of the hostility that had once resided within them. They remained a dark and disturbing presence in Arthur's studio, a constant reminder of the entity that had haunted his family for generations.

Only time would reveal the actual consequences of Arthur's desperate act. Had he banished the entity for good, or had he merely pressed pause on a cosmic horror that would return with a vengeance? As he moved forward, he could only hope that the nightmare was truly over and that the cursed painting would no longer haunt him and his family.

As weeks turned into months, Arthur continued to live with the shattered remains of the cursed painting in his studio. He had considered disposing of them entirely, but an inexplicable reluctance held him back. It was as if some of him feared that destroying every trace of the painting might provoke the entity's wrath in ways he couldn't predict.

He immersed himself in researching ancient rituals and protective spells, seeking any means to ensure that the eldritch horror would never return. His obsession with preventing the entity's resurgence bordered on madness, but he couldn't shake the feeling that the nightmare was far from over.

The room seemed limbo, caught between the horrors of its past and an uncertain future. The walls once witnessed unspeakable terrors.

There was a palpable sense of anticipation, as though the room held its breath, ready to confront whatever darkness lay ahead.

Unsettling dreams still plagued Arthur's nights, though they no longer reached the depths of cosmic horror he had once experienced. The entity's presence remained a constant, a shadow that loomed over his subconscious. It whispered secrets and incantations in the forgotten tongues of eldritch knowledge, promises of power and enlightenment that danced on the fringes of his understanding.

With each night, Arthur's dreams continued to escalate, albeit to a lesser degree. The landscapes he traversed were surreal and dreamlike, filled with indescribable colors and otherworldly vistas. The entity beckoned from the shadows, its voice a sinister echo that clawed at his psyche. It promised forbidden knowledge, but the price it demanded was Arthur's very soul.

Arthur became increasingly obsessed with deciphering the entity's secrets as time passed. He sought ancient texts and consulted with scholars of the arcane, all in a desperate attempt to understand

and control the eldritch horror that had plagued his family for generations.

The shattered remains of the cursed painting served as a constant reminder of the evil force that had once resided within it. They were a haunting presence, a testament to the horrors that had unfolded in that room. Arthur couldn't escape the feeling that the entity was not truly defeated and merely bided its time, waiting for the right moment to return.

The room had borne witness to so much suffering and had become a place of uncertainty and trepidation. It was a chamber of secrets where the boundaries between the real and the supernatural were blurred. The atmosphere seemed to hold the weight of cosmic dread as if it had absorbed the hostility that had once permeated its corners.

In the end, Arthur Blackwood's life became a constant struggle to prevent the entity's return and protect his family from the curse that had haunted them for centuries. The shattered remnants of the cursed painting were a constant reminder of the darkness that had once consumed his ancestors, and he would stop at nothing to ensure that it never claimed another victim.

And so, the room that had once been a chamber of madness now stood as a battleground, where one man confronted the horrors of his family's legacy and a malevolent force lurking in the shadows, waiting for its chance to return.

Part IV

Epilogue: A Sinister Deal

Chapter 30

The Art Distributor

The Cursed Canvas

Amelia Hartley, the enigmatic art distributor, had cultivated a reputation as a maverick in art. Her uncanny ability to unearth rare and provocative works that challenged conventional aesthetics had earned her both admiration and envy within the art community. Yet, when rumors of the cursed painting reached her ears, it was unlike anything she had ever encountered.

The tales that swirled around the cursed canvas were a bewildering blend of fascination and dread. The mere mention of its dark reputation sent shivers down the spines of even the most seasoned art connoisseurs. For Amelia, this was a mystery that demanded her full attention, an enigma that beckoned her adventurous spirit.

As she delved deeper into the legends and folklore surrounding the painting, she couldn't help but feel a growing sense of intrigue. The accounts of the curse's effects on its various owners were too compelling to ignore, and they filled her with a sense of foreboding that thrilled her inquisitive soul. This was not just a work of art; it was a force that defied rational explanation.

The Cursed Canvas

Amelia's relentless research eventually led her to Arthur Blackwood, the last owner who had managed to survive the painting's evil influence. They met in a dimly lit café, where the weight of the curse's history hung heavily in the air. The conversations unfolded were marked by hesitation and caution, for both knew the perils of dealing with the cursed canvas.

After much discussion, they arrived at a peculiar agreement. Amelia proposed creating limited-edition prints of the cursed painting, believing this would be a way to expose the entity's dark influence while maintaining a degree of control. Arthur, caught between his desire to confront the curse and the ever-present fear of its consequences, eventually consented to the arrangement. It was a decision that would lead them deeper into the enigmatic world of cosmic horror.

The project began, and the studio, once a place of nightmarish descent, was transformed into a collaboration site. Amelia and Arthur meticulously worked to recreate the image of the cursed painting, the oppressive aura of the room enveloping them with every brush stroke. It was as if the studio had absorbed the hostility of the original painting and was now radiating it back into the world through their creation.

The limited-edition prints that emerged from their joint effort were haunting. Each print captured the essence of the cursed painting's eldritch horror and malice and carried an aura of sinister allure. Collectors and enthusiasts were drawn to their eerie beauty, and the knowledge of the painting's dark history only added to their desirability. It was as if the cursed canvas had found a new way to trap those who came into contact with its image, this time through the allure of artistry rather than direct possession.

As the prints found their way into the hands of collectors, the room, which had once been a chamber of madness, stood as a silent sentinel of the sinister deal that had taken place. It was as if the entity's influence still lingered in the very walls, weaving its dark threads through the art world and ensnaring all who dared to possess a piece of its malice. The cursed canvas's dark odyssey had found a new path, and its story was far from over. The studio, now a place of collaboration, continued to witness the entwining of art and cosmic horror, an unholy alliance that defied the boundaries of the known

world.

Chapter 31

The Collector's Obsession

The Cursed Canvas

In the dimly lit room of Richard Langley's secluded mansion, the art collector reveled in the glory of his latest acquisition. He had always been drawn to the unconventional and the mysterious, seeking out pieces of art that carried a dark reputation. With its sinister allure, the limited-edition print of the cursed painting was irresistible to him.

As he carefully hung the print in the opulent gallery of his mansion, a subtle unease settled in the room. The air seemed to thicken, and the atmosphere witnessed the eerie transformation. The image of the grotesque entity on the print pulsed with a bizarre life of its own, and the coldness seemed to emanate from it. It was as though the cursed canvas held secrets that defied human comprehension.

The first night the print adorned the gallery, Richard's sleep was hijacked by vivid and unsettling nightmares. He found himself wandering through eldritch landscapes, where colors defied human description, and the air weighed heavy with impending doom. The entity, the same eldritch horror that had tormented Arthur Blackwood and others before him, beckoned from the shadows. It whispered forbidden secrets in forgotten tongues, promising power and knowledge beyond imagination in exchange for his allegiance.

In the days that followed, Richard's obsession with the print deepened. He couldn't tear his eyes away from the grotesque image, and the whispers of the entity echoed in his mind, offering tantalizing promises. The compulsion to possess more prints, to surround himself with the cursed image, consumed him.

The room where the print hung had witnessed Richard's descent into madness. His daily life was now filled with subtle and ominous occurrences. Objects moved mysteriously, as if of their own accord, and strange symbols, like ancient hieroglyphs, manifested on the walls. The room itself had become a canvas for cosmic secrets. Shadows danced in the corners of his vision, and the air held an ominous chill he could not ignore.

The cursed image had found a new host in Richard Langley, and the curse's persistence was undeniable in the sinister occurrences that now infiltrated every facet of his world. He had unwittingly invited cosmic horror into his life, and the consequences of his obsession were becoming increasingly apparent.

The Cursed Canvas

As Richard Langley's life descended into a nightmarish spiral, the curse's malevolence continued to seep into his existence. The sinister allure of the cursed painting had ensnared him, and there was no escape from the relentless grip of the entity that now plagued his days and tormented his nights.

The very fabric of Richard's mansion seemed to warp and twist in response to the cursed presence. Shadows lengthened into sinister shapes, and whispers of forgotten languages echoed through its grand halls. The once-stately home had become a theater of dread, where cosmic forces conspired to drive him to the brink of madness.

The cursed print that adorned his gallery became the focal point of his existence. Richard's obsession with it deepened to the point where he could spend hours gazing at the grotesque image. The entity's whispers grew more insistent, promising dark power and esoteric knowledge in return for his devotion.

The symbols that had appeared on the gallery walls were no longer confined to that room. They spread like a contagion, crawling across the mansion's surfaces as if the walls had become infected with the curse. Richard couldn't escape the feeling that his home was no longer his own, that he had become a prisoner within its haunted confines.

The mansion's once-elegant corridors and grand rooms now held a sinister secret. The air was heavy with an oppressive aura, and an unnatural chill permeated the walls. Shadows seemed to move with an evil intent, whispering secrets that danced on the fringes of his understanding.

Richard began to catch glimpses of the entity in the darkness of these haunted hallways. It would manifest as a shadowy figure, its eyes filled with an ancient enmity, always just beyond his reach. The mansion seemed to rejoice in the evil spectacle, its walls pulsating with an eerie, otherworldly rhythm as if they were rejoicing in the chaos and horror that had permeated their once tranquil corners.

Richard Langley's sanity continued to crumble in his relentless pursuit of the entity's favor. He could no longer distinguish between his desires and the sinister whispers guiding his actions. The cursed print had become an all-consuming obsession, and Richard had willingly surrendered himself to the entity's insidious influence.

As Richard Langley's obsession deepened, the cursed print seemed to take on a life of its own. The grotesque image appeared to pulse with otherworldly energy as if it were a portal to an eldritch realm beyond human comprehension. The room in which it hung quivered with unnatural power as if it were a conscious entity that reveled in the descent of its latest victim into madness.

Each passing day further blurred the line between Richard and the entity, and the cursed image served as the conduit for their unholy communion. Shadows danced around the gallery. A sinister ballet mirrored the creeping malevolence that had become integral to his existence.

The symbols on the walls spread like a plague, crawling across the mansion's surfaces, and the air grew thicker with an oppressive aura. Richard's mind became a battlefield, where his desires clashed with the entity's demands, a relentless struggle that seemed to have no end.

One fateful night, as he stood before the cursed print, Richard felt an irresistible compulsion to pick up a brush and continue the entity's grotesque image. His hand moved with a fevered intensity, guided by an external force, an evil presence that reveled in his descent into madness.

With each stroke, the entity on the print grew more vivid and vicious, as if it were clawing its way into the waking world. The room seemed to pulsate with an unnatural energy, and the air was thick with a palpable malice as if it were savoring the unholy act of creation. The cursed image and its host were locked in a perverse dance of creation and destruction, and the mansion bore witness to the ultimate confrontation between the collector and the eldritch entity.

As Richard's sanity continued to unravel, he knew that a confrontation with the entity was inevitable. The room, which had witnessed so many nightmarish visions, was now a place of unspeakable dread. The cursed print seemed to radiate an unholy energy, and the grotesque image of the entity pulsed with life.

The Cursed Canvas

One night, as Richard worked tirelessly in his gallery, he sensed the entity's presence within the print growing stronger. The air grew heavy with an oppressive aura, and a sense of foreboding filled the room. The atmosphere seemed to tighten as if it were bracing for the imminent arrival of cosmic horror.

Then, in a pivotal moment, as Richard stood before the cursed print, he witnessed the entity within it shift and contort. It was as if the eldritch abomination was preparing to breach the boundaries of the print and step into the waking world. The grotesque image writhed and undulated, taking on a dreadful life of its own.

The room itself seemed to rejoice in the evil spectacle that was unfolding. Its walls pulsated with an eerie, otherworldly rhythm, as if they were delighting in the chaos and horror that had permeated their once tranquil corners. The gallery, once a place of inspiration, was now a theater of madness, and its walls bore witness to the nightmarish transformation.

The entity fully emerged from the print with a final, chilling crescendo. It materialized with a sinister grace, its form contorting and shifting as it crossed the threshold into the waking world. Its eyes, filled with an ancient enmity, locked onto Richard, and the room quivered with an unnatural energy. The air was heavy with palpable malice, as if it were savoring the moment, and a maddening cacophony of otherworldly whispers filled the room.

The line between art and reality had dissolved entirely in that nightmarish moment. The entity that had once resided within the confines of the cursed print was now a tangible, horrifying presence in Richard Langley's world. The gallery, which had witnessed so many nightmarish visions, was now host to the ultimate confrontation between the collector and the eldritch entity.

The entity reached out with elongated, shadowy limbs, and its eyes locked onto Richard. The room, the site of so much suffering, seemed to hold its breath as the two figures faced each other.

With a chilling grace, the entity moved closer to Richard, its shadowy appendages reaching out. The room quivered with an otherworldly energy, and the air was thick with an oppressive aura. It was a moment of reckoning, a showdown between the cursed print and the last owner.

Richard felt a surge of dread and despair as the entity's appendages wrapped around him. The room was filled with a cacophony of otherworldly whispers, a chorus of ancient tongues clawed at the edges of his sanity. The artist's last moments were a nightmarish dance of creation and destruction, leading him to descend into the abyss from which there was no return.

The room fell into an eerie silence, the oppressive darkness lingering as a testament to the unholy events that had transpired. Once again unclaimed, the cursed print held the essence of its latest victim, ready to find a new host and continue its reign of terror.

Chapter 32

The Art Enthusiast's Descent

The Cursed Canvas

Marissa Turner, a dedicated art enthusiast with a penchant for the unconventional and the mysterious, had always been drawn to the darker corners of the art world. When she learned of the limited-edition prints of the cursed painting, her curiosity got the better of her. She couldn't resist the allure of owning a piece with such a sinister reputation, so she acquired one for her private collection.

As Marissa proudly hung the print on the walls of her art-filled apartment, she immediately noticed a subtle but undeniable shift in the atmosphere. The room seemed to carry heavy weight, as if it held the secrets of countless nightmares within its confines. The image of the grotesque entity, seemingly frozen on the canvas, appeared to move when she wasn't looking directly at it, a trick of the mind that gnawed at her sanity.

Night after night, Marissa found herself plagued by vivid and unsettling nightmares. She would awaken in cold sweats, her mind haunted by the surreal landscapes she had traversed in her dreams. It was as though the cursed entity had taken residence in her subconscious, guiding her through eldritch realms with its whispers in long-forgotten tongues. The entity beckoned from the shadows, offering forbidden knowledge and power that tempted her beyond reason. Marissa's once peaceful slumber had become a descent into the abyss, with each night's dreams revealing more profound layers of cosmic horror.

The compulsion to acquire more prints of the cursed painting grew stronger daily. Marissa's art collection, once a source of joy and inspiration, had transformed into a gallery of cosmic horror. The cursed image had become an obsession, its grotesque depiction of the entity occupying more and more space within her mind. The line between her passion for art and the curse's relentless grip blurred, and she felt the entity's presence like a tightening noose around her soul.

After Marissa hung the print in her room, strange things began. Objects shifted mysteriously when she wasn't looking, giving her an eerie feeling. She started hearing faint whispers in the dead of night that echoed in her mind, whispering secrets best left unheard. The cursed image had trapped her, and it was evident from the unsettling happenings that haunted her life.

The Cursed Canvas

The cursed print had irrevocably altered Marissa's once-peaceful existence. What had initially seemed like an intriguing addition to her collection had become a source of torment, and she couldn't escape the feeling that she had invited an evil force into her life. With its grotesque entity, the cursed painting had claimed another victim. Marissa Turner was trapped in its relentless grip, her world forever altered by the sinister allure of the artwork she had acquired.

As the curse tightened its grip on Marissa, she found herself unable to resist the insidious pull of the entity within the print. The nightmares continued to escalate, each one a descent into more profound, more intricate layers of cosmic horror. The entity's presence, once a distant specter, now clung to her like an evil shadow, whispering secrets and incantations into the recesses of her mind.

In her obsession, Marissa became increasingly isolated from the outside world. Her friends and family grew concerned as they noticed her deteriorating mental state, but she was unwilling to part with the cursed print that had trapped her so completely. She became consumed by the desire to possess more prints, to spread the curse further, and her once-thriving social life dwindled into nothingness.

The room where the print hung had become a place of dread, its atmosphere thick with foreboding. Subtle, ominous occurrences were now a part of Marissa's daily life. Objects would move independently, and strange symbols began appearing on the walls. Shadows seemed to dance in the corners of her vision, and the room quivered with an unnatural energy. It was as though the walls had become complicit in the unholy act of creation, and Marissa's life had become a theater of madness.

As Marissa's obsession with the cursed painting deepened, her reflection in the canvases seemed to contort and shift, mirroring the madness that consumed her. She could no longer distinguish where the artist ended, and the entity began. The line between her identity and the eldritch entity had blurred, and she was locked in a perverse dance of creation and destruction. The room itself had become an evil entity, seemingly complicit in this unholy act of creation. The air was thick with an oppressive aura, and the atmosphere seemed to rejoice in the chaos and horror permeating its once-tranquil corners.

The Cursed Canvas

Marissa's friends and family watched in despair as she spiraled into madness, helpless to intervene as she descended further into the curse's clutches. The cursed image had found a new victim in Marissa Turner, and the curse's persistence was evident in the sinister occurrences that plagued her life. It was a nightmare she couldn't awaken, and the cursed print, once a mere piece of art, had become the source of her torment.

Chapter 33

The Curator's Obsession

The Cursed Canvas

Evelyn Grant, a highly respected art curator renowned for her discerning taste and unwavering dedication to preserving artistic legacies, was drawn to the enigmatic allure of the limited-edition prints of the cursed painting. In the art world, her name was synonymous with the appreciation of true craftsmanship and safeguarding cultural treasures. She couldn't resist the temptation when the opportunity arose to acquire one of these prints for her private collection.

As the cursed print took place among the carefully curated works in her collection, Evelyn immediately sensed an undeniable change in her surroundings. The air within the room seemed to thicken as if it bore the weight of ancient secrets and long-forgotten horrors. The space took on a surreal, unsettling ambiance as if it had become a gateway to realms beyond human comprehension. The image of the grotesque entity on the print appeared to shift and contort, its malicious form seemingly mocking her from within its frame.

Night after night, Evelyn's sleep became a theater of cosmic dread. She found herself trapped within eldritch landscapes that defied all description, where the colors were otherworldly, and the air was laden with impending doom. The entity, the eldritch horror that had tormented so many before her, beckoned from the shadows. It whispered forbidden secrets and incantations in long-forgotten tongues, offering promises of power and knowledge in exchange for her unwavering devotion.

The compulsion to possess more prints of the cursed painting grew every day. Once a sanctuary of artistic pursuit and a testament to her unwavering love for art, Evelyn's studio was transformed into a nightmarish labyrinth. Within its confines, the boundaries between the art she cherished and the eldritch visions that now tormented her blurred into obscurity. She could no longer distinguish between her passion for art and the curse's insidious grip.

Subtle but ominous occurrences began to plague Evelyn's life. Paintings in her collection seemed to shift and change when she wasn't looking, their subjects appearing to move with an energy of their own. Strange symbols, ancient and mysterious, began to manifest on the walls of her studio as if they were messages from the beyond. Shadows danced in the corners of her vision, and faint and unsettling whispers echoed through the room as though the atmosphere was infused with an evil presence.

The cursed image had claimed yet another victim, and the curse's persistence was evident in the eerie happenings that now permeated Evelyn's world. She had ventured into the realm of the eldritch, lured by the allure of the cursed painting, and now she was trapped in its relentless grip. Her life had become a nightmarish descent into the abyss, and the curse's insidious influence showed no signs of waning.

As the cursed image continued to haunt Evelyn, its sinister presence manifested in even more unsettling ways. The grotesque entity on the print seemed to move, its monstrous features shifting and contorting as if striving to break free from its two-dimensional prison. This unsettling phenomenon was not a mere trick of the eye; the curse that permeated the image had given it a semblance of life within the realm of the living.

The nights grew increasingly tormenting for Evelyn. Dreams of cosmic horror plagued her sleep, and the entity beckoned to her from the shadows. It whispered in a cacophony of forgotten tongues, each utterance a chilling promise of power and forbidden knowledge. The compulsion to acquire more prints of the cursed painting, to immerse herself further in its eldritch allure, grew stronger with each passing day.

Evelyn's once-sacred studio had become a place of madness. The walls bore witness to her frantic attempts to understand the cursed image, covered in intricate patterns and symbols that seemed to defy human comprehension. The line between her passion for art and the curse's relentless grip had blurred entirely, and she could not escape the all-encompassing darkness that now held her in its thrall.

Subtle but ominous occurrences continued to plague her existence. Paintings throughout her collection shifted and changed of their own accord as if they were attempting to communicate with her. Strange symbols, etched in blood-red hues, appeared on the walls, cryptic messages from the eldritch depths. The shadows in the room seemed to take on a life of their own, twisting and writhing in ways that defied the laws of nature.

The Cursed Canvas

As Evelyn's life descended into chaos, the cursed image's sinister grip on her world showed no signs of relenting. She had unwittingly become the latest victim of the cursed painting's insatiable appetite for fear and souls, ensnared in a nightmare from which there seemed no escape.

Chapter 34

The Art Dealer's Avarice

The Cursed Canvas

Charles Whitman, a well-known art dealer with a penchant for rare and controversial pieces, couldn't resist the allure of the limited-edition prints of the cursed painting. The print represented a lucrative opportunity to him, and he acquired it to sell it to the highest bidder.

As he proudly displayed the print in his high-end art gallery, the room seemed to undergo a subtle transformation. The air carried an unsettling weight, and the image of the grotesque entity appeared to shift and contort as if it were clawing its way out of the frame.

Charles' nights became plagued by vivid and unsettling nightmares. He wandered through surreal landscapes, where colors defied description, and the air was pregnant with impending doom. The entity beckoned from the shadows, whispering secrets and incantations in forgotten tongues, offering promises of untold wealth and power.

The compulsion to acquire more prints of the cursed painting became all-consuming. Charles's art gallery, once a place of prestige, was transformed into a chamber of eldritch allure, where the boundaries between art and the curse blurred into obscurity. He could not distinguish his desire for wealth from the curse's relentless grip.

Ominous occurrences gradually seeped into Charles' life. Valuable artworks were inexplicably devalued, strange symbols appeared on the walls, and unsettling whispers echoed in the gallery's corridors. The cursed image had claimed another victim, and the curse's persistence was palpable in the eerie incidents that now tainted Charles' world.

In his relentless pursuit of profit, Charles Whitman had unwittingly invited cosmic horror into his life. The cursed image had not only devalued the art within his gallery but had also tainted the very essence of his professional success. He had become a pawn in an evil game, a victim of the cursed painting's insatiable appetite for fear and souls.

The eerie incidents in his gallery became increasingly unsettling. Valuable artworks that had once commanded high prices on the market suddenly lost their value. Clients who had previously regarded him with reverence now eyed his gallery suspiciously.

The Cursed Canvas

Ancient and mysterious, strange symbols began to manifest on the gallery's walls as if they were messages from an evil presence that sought to communicate with him. The whispers that echoed in the corridors were faint but chilling, their source remaining elusive, but their message unmistakably sinister.

The cursed image, which Charles had initially seen as a source of potential profit, had trapped him in its relentless grip. The curse's persistence was palpable in the eerie incidents that now tainted his world, as the boundaries between art and the eldritch blurred, leaving him a victim of the cursed painting's insatiable appetite for fear and souls.

Chapter 35

The Art Historian's Investigation

The Cursed Canvas

Dr. Elizabeth Simmons, a renowned art historian known for her rigorous research and dedication to uncovering hidden stories in the art world, had been intrigued by the rumors of the cursed painting's prints. With a curiosity fueled by her love for art and history, she investigated the truth behind the dark legend.

Upon acquiring a limited-edition print, Elizabeth felt the atmosphere of her study subtly shift. The room seemed to bear the weight of untold secrets, and the image of the grotesque entity on the print appeared to pulse with a strange vitality as if it held cosmic truths.

Each night, her sleep was disrupted by vivid and unsettling nightmares. She wandered through surreal landscapes, where the colors defied human description, and the air was laden with impending doom. The entity beckoned from the shadows, whispering secrets and incantations in forgotten tongues, offering forbidden knowledge.

The compulsion to delve deeper into the cursed painting's history grew stronger daily. Once a sanctuary of academic pursuit, Elizabeth's study transformed into a chamber of enigmatic allure, where the boundaries between art and the curse blurred beyond recognition. She could not distinguish her scholarly curiosity from the curse's insistent allure.

Subtle, ominous occurrences began to intrude into Elizabeth's life. Her research notes seemed to rearrange themselves, unfamiliar symbols appeared on her pages, and whispers of forgotten tongues echoed in her ears. The cursed image had trapped her, and the curse's persistence was unmistakable in the eerie incidents that now infiltrated Elizabeth's world.

As Dr. Elizabeth Simmons delved deeper into the cursed painting's history, she found herself on a path that led to darkness. Her once scholarly pursuits had transformed into a relentless obsession fueled by the enigmatic allure of the cursed image. The room where the print hung, which had once been a place of academic discovery, had become a realm of unsettling secrets.

Night after night, the nightmares grew more intricate and horrifying, pulling her further into the abyss. The entity's presence had permeated her very being, whispering forbidden knowledge and secrets that gnawed at the edges of her sanity. The line between scholarly curiosity and a dark compulsion had blurred, leaving her unable to distinguish one from the other.

Subtle, ominous occurrences continued to infiltrate Elizabeth's life. Research notes, meticulously organized, now shifted and rearranged themselves as if driven by an unseen hand. Symbols, ancient and mystifying, began to manifest on her pages, defying her attempts at deciphering their meaning. Whispers of forgotten tongues, echoing in the quiet corners of her study, seemed to mock her, offering cryptic messages that eluded her understanding.

Once a subject of investigation, the cursed image had trapped her in its relentless grip. The curse's persistence was unmistakable in the eerie incidents that now infiltrated every aspect of her life as she struggled to navigate the thin line between scholarly pursuit and the seductive pull of cosmic horror.

As Elizabeth delved deeper into the cursed painting's history, she unearthed dark secrets. The origins of the curse, the tormented souls it had claimed, and the evil entity it contained became the focal points of her obsessive research. Once a curiosity, the cursed image now held her in its thrall.

Each night, her sleep was a descent into nightmarish realms where eldritch landscapes defied the laws of nature. The colors were beyond human comprehension, and the air bore the weight of impending doom. The entity beckoned from the shadows, offering forbidden knowledge and promises of power that tempted her beyond reason.

The compulsion to uncover the curse's secrets grew stronger every day. Her study, once a place of scholarly dedication, had become a chamber of cosmic horrors. The boundaries between her academic pursuits and the curse's relentless allure blurred, and she felt the entity's presence like an ever-tightening noose around her soul.

Ominous occurrences continued to infiltrate Elizabeth's life. Research notes and documents shifted as if guided by unseen hands, rearranging themselves to taunt her. Symbols of arcane significance appeared on her pages, defying her attempts to decipher their meaning.

Whispers of forgotten tongues filled her ears, offering cryptic messages that eluded her understanding.

The cursed image had trapped her, and the curse's persistence was evident in the unsettling incidents that now infiltrated every aspect of her existence. Elizabeth walked a precarious line between scholarly inquiry and the seductive pull of cosmic horror, unable to escape the relentless grip of the cursed painting's dark legacy.

Chapter 36

The Unending Horror

The Cursed Canvas

Like a vicious contagion, the cursed prints continued to increase, silently spreading their sinister influence. They found their way into the hands of individuals from all walks of life, each drawn by their curiosity or fascination with the enigmatic legend.

As the prints adorned the walls of various collectors' homes, the rooms they inhabited seemed to transform. An uncanny atmosphere settled over these spaces, an unshakable feeling that something beyond human comprehension now resided within. The image of the grotesque entity on the print appeared to possess an alarming vitality as if it held a cosmic secret that yearned to be unraveled.

Night after night, those who possessed the cursed prints were plagued by the same vivid and unsettling nightmares. They wandered through landscapes that defied description, where colors were surreal, and the air bore the unmistakable weight of impending doom. The entity beckoned from the shadows, whispering forbidden secrets in long-forgotten tongues, offering untold power and knowledge in exchange for their allegiance.

The Cursed Canvas

The compulsion to acquire more prints grew stronger daily, like a relentless undertow pulling them deeper into the abyss. Their homes, once places of comfort and solace, were transformed into chambers of eldritch allure, where the boundaries between art and the curse blurred beyond recognition. They could not distinguish their desire for the prints from the curse's relentless grip.

Ominous occurrences became a part of their daily lives, a constant reminder of the entity's pervasive presence. Objects moved mysteriously, symbols appeared on the walls, and faint, unsettling whispers echoed in the stillness of the night. The cursed prints ensnared those who possessed them, and the curse's persistence was palpable in the eerie incidents that now infiltrated their worlds.

The cursed prints had become a conduit for cosmic terror, a gateway to the eldritch horrors lurking just beyond reality's veil. With each new victim, the curse's reach extended, its insidious legacy perpetuating the nightmare. The final revelation was clear: the curse remained unbroken, and the cosmic horror it embodied was an eternal force, leaving behind a trail of madness and death, transcending time and space. It was a horror that persisted, an unending nightmare, and those who gazed upon the cursed prints were forever bound to its dark and dreadful embrace.

The curse seemed to be an ever-present force, and its horrors would continue to unfold in the lives of those who dared to seek its dark allure. The nightmare persisted, transcending generations, and those who came into contact with the prints were forever marked by the cosmic horror that clung to them like a shadow. The curse's unending reach served as a grim reminder that some terrors were not bound by time or space, and the evil entity within the prints would forever whisper its forbidden secrets to those who ventured too close, leaving a legacy of madness and death in its wake.

Epilogue

The Enigma's Echo

The Cursed Canvas

As the years passed, the enigmatic prints of the cursed painting continued their clandestine journey through the art world, a sinister legend known to only a select few. The true nature of the existing entity within them remained as elusive as ever, its enigma deepening with each passing generation. Those who unknowingly acquired the prints were drawn into a web of cosmic horror, their lives forever altered.

Each print carried the echoes of the original cursed painting's dark history, but its hostility had evolved, taking on a life of its own. The grotesque entity depicted in the prints seemed to shift and contort as if it were yearning to break free from the confines of the paper and canvas. Its form pulsed with an eerie vitality as if it held the secrets to an otherworldly dimension, a dimension that threatened to engulf all who dared to approach it.

The nightmares that plagued the print owners persisted, becoming more vivid and disturbing as time passed. The dreamscapes they traversed defied human comprehension, with colors beyond description and an air heavy with impending doom. The entity beckoned from the shadows, whispering secrets and incantations in forgotten tongues, seducing those who listened with promises of forbidden knowledge and power. Once isolated to the realm of sleep, the nightmares began to bleed into the waking world, blurring the lines of reality and dreams.

The compulsion to acquire more prints of the cursed painting intensified daily, an insidious pull that blurred the line between desire and obsession. The rooms where the images were displayed became places of eerie occurrences, where objects moved independently, strange symbols manifested on the walls, and shadows danced in the corners of vision. Those who gazed upon the prints found themselves entrapped in a web of compulsion and dread, unable to escape the sinister allure.

The curse's legacy persisted, claiming one victim after another, each trapped by its dark allure. The enigma remained unsolved, a mystery that defied comprehension, and the cosmic horror endured, patiently waiting for the next unsuspecting soul to be drawn into its web. The prints themselves, seemingly innocuous yet harboring an unfathomable darkness, were the conduits through which the curse manifested its relentless grip on the world.

Ultimately, the cursed prints stood as a testament to an enduring enigma, a haunting reminder that some secrets were meant to remain hidden, and some horrors were destined to remain forever beyond the grasp of human understanding. While the world turned its attention elsewhere, oblivious to the evil force that lurked within the prints, the legacy of unanswered questions and the ever-present sense of dread endured, casting a long shadow over the unsuspecting souls who would come into contact with the cursed prints in the future.

The enigma persisted, a question mark that refused to yield its answers, and the cosmic horror, as old as time itself, continued its unending descent into the minds of those who dared to seek its mysteries. The curse remained, an invincible force that defied explanation, and its echoes would continue reverberating through the corridors of history, leaving a trail of darkness in their wake.

Afterword

By

Magnum Tenebrosum

The Cursed Canvas

Dear Curious Soul,

As the ink dries on the pages of this eldritch tome, I am compelled to share some reflections on the journey you have just undertaken. The cursed painting's tale, a chronicle of cosmic horror that I had the dubious honor of chronicling, is not merely a work of fiction; it is a descent into enigmatic and inescapable darkness.

You, the reader, have ventured into a world where the boundary between reality and nightmare is as thin as gossamer, and the eldritch forces that lie beyond our understanding grasp your soul. You have become a witness to the relentless, timeless horror that defies explanation, a silent observer in the grand theater of malevolence.

The curse that binds this narrative is no mere construct of words; it is an ever-persistent entity, a shadowy force that seizes those who dare to peer into the abyss. It hungers for fear and despair and seeks to sow the seeds of cosmic terror in the fertile soil of your imagination.

The cursed painting, which has claimed the lives and minds of many, is a vessel for something far more ancient and dreadful than the human mind can comprehend. It is a portal to the realms of the unknown, and its echoes reach far beyond the confines of this tale. Its tendrils reach the darkest corners of your mind, where the horrors it conceals continue to linger, lurking in the shadows of your consciousness.

As you close this book and re-enter the world you once knew, remember that you may never truly escape the curse's insidious influence. The boundary between fiction and reality blurs, and the sinister whispers of the cursed painting will haunt your thoughts, dreams, and darkest fears.

The curse's persistence is relentless, and its echoes may manifest when you least expect them. It may reveal itself in the unsettling creak of a door, the unexplained movement of an object, or the chilling whisper of a forgotten language in the dead of night. You may catch glimpses of the grotesque entity in the corner of your eye, its eldritch form lingering in the periphery of your vision.

Ultimately, I offer you no solace, no respite from the lingering dread. The cursed painting remains a malevolent sentinel of fear, and its influence may continue to seep into your reality. You have become a part of this cursed narrative, and its enigma now resides within you.

With the knowledge that you have been forever touched by the eldritch and the enigmatic, I bid you farewell, dear reader, and may you find peace in the darkness that now dwells within you.

Yours in cosmic dread,

Magnum Tenebrosum

Milton Keynes UK
Ingram Content Group UK Ltd.
UKHW020924231123
433129UK00016B/1027